He needed her friendship.

Anything else was dangerous. Besides, she was like a sister. They'd survived acne, cafeteria pizza and countless fights over the remote.

"Listen, I'm happy to see you, but coming to Alto is a bad plan. The conditions aren't what you're used to and—"

"And you're afraid I'll tumble right on into love with you again. It's okay. I'm smarter now than I was then. I realize you were right. We are good friends, and that doesn't mean we should be anything more. Don't worry."

She squeezed his hand.

"Friends. That's all. Now help me show your sister and Jen that they don't know everything they think they do. Take me to Alto. I'll stay until you're coming back to Lima. I might even be able to help."

Dear Reader,

Traveling the world from my couch has been a hobby of mine for a long time. As a young girl, I would check out the coffee-table photography books of Ireland and Scotland and dream of castles. In junior high, a project on Barcelona led me to the travel-guide shelves. Since then, I've carefully planned every vacation I've taken and dreamed big dreams about the ones I've yet to manage. What I didn't know then, when I was studying big pictures of places large and small, was how travel could change the way I see the world and myself.

In *Winner Takes All*, Stephanie Yates learns this lesson after she takes a trip to Peru on a dare. Her best friend's older brother is making a difference and making a life in the Andes Mountains. Once Stephanie has a chance to show what she can do, she understands that she's limited only by her own fear. The conditions are nothing like home. And neither is the satisfaction she feels with each new adventure. I hope you enjoy seeing some of Peru and meeting Stephanie and Daniel.

If you'd like to know more about my books and what's coming next, enter fun giveaways, or meet my dog, Jack, please visit me at cherylharperbooks.com. You can sign up for my newsletter, too. I'm also on Facebook (CherylHarperRomance) and Twitter (@CherylHarperBks). I'd love to chat!

Cheryl Harper

HEARTWARMING

Winner Takes All

———

Cheryl Harper

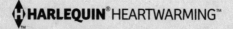

Recycling programs
for this product may
not exist in your area.

ISBN-13: 978-0-373-36729-0

Winner Takes All

Printed in U.S.A.

Cheryl Harper discovered her love for books and words as a little girl, thanks to a mother who made countless library trips and an introduction to Laura Ingalls Wilder's Little House stories. Whether it's the prairie, the American West, Regency England or Earth a hundred years in the future, Cheryl enjoys strong characters who make her laugh. Now Cheryl spends her days searching for the right words while she stares out the window and her dog, Jack, snoozes beside her. And she considers herself very lucky to do so.

For more information about Cheryl's books, visit her online at cherylharperbooks.com or follow her on Twitter, @cherylharperbks.

Books by Cheryl Harper

Harlequin Heartwarming

A Minute on the Lips
The Bluebird Bet

Visit the Author Profile page
at Harlequin.com for more titles.

Many thanks to my editor, Dana Grimaldi,
for the questions, suggestions and encouragement
that make my books so much better.

CHAPTER ONE

"So he reached across the table and took my hand—" Stephanie dropped into her normal spot on the couch with a huff "—and told me how much he appreciated my help with Stacy. He never would've patched things up with her without my *friendship*."

"That's Brian's loss," Rebecca said. She eased down beside Stephanie and fluffed her ruffled apron over the sundress she'd worn to celebrate the last day of school. Rebecca offered Stephanie a plate of chocolate chip cookies. "You did the right thing. It's not bad to be such a good friend."

"But he was my *date*." Stephanie took a cookie in each hand and glumly bit into one of them. "The dating service was supposed to change this talent I have for converting every romantic possibility into another guy who values my *advice*." She'd signed up believing she needed to broaden her horizons, get out of Holly Heights. Apparently her skill had nothing to do with the city limits.

"Some people can add ridiculously large sums in their heads. Others can play concertos without sheet music. You can make a friend out of anyone. That's handy, right? People depend on you." Rebecca nodded encouragingly as she passed the plate to Jen, the third of the Holy Horrors. Rebecca's older brother had given them that name the first summer they'd dogged his footsteps.

Stephanie took a bite of the cookie in her left hand to stop herself from rolling her eyes in response.

Jen snorted. Of the three of them, she was most likely to call it like she saw it and let the chips fall where they may. "You should take a film crew on your next date. Then we can evaluate your skills, do some careful study of how you keep doing this."

"Great idea. Wish we'd thought of it years ago. We could even do an educational video for people like me." If there were any others who managed to convert chemistry to camaraderie with a hardly perceptible fizzle.

"Enough of Brian and his baggage." Jen shook her head, her dark hair swinging thanks to the asymmetrical bob. "He was safe. So was the last guy... What was his name? Andrew? And the one before him and the one before that. It's like they're all beige. Not a single one stands out. I'm starting to think that's why you like them."

That was hard to argue with. "Safe is good. Boring but good." Her mother might not have said it in exactly the same way, but there was no doubt where Stephanie had picked up that philosophy.

"We aren't going to challenge you there," Rebecca said. "What Holly Heights lacks in excitement, it certainly makes up for in predictability." She pointed at each of them in their usual spots in her living room. Jen was sprawled across an armchair wiggling one foot with nervous energy, and Stephanie was curled up on the couch. With a cookie in each hand. "But it doesn't seem like safe makes you happy lately."

"I thought searching outside Holly Heights would work. Here there's no mystery, none of that anticipation. Maybe I need to try... I

don't know…rodeo clowns or stuntmen or…"
She couldn't even *think* of a third crazy example. How depressing.

But she could easily imagine her mother's wrinkled brow if she ever managed to
track down a stuntman and bring him home
to dinner.

"Forget him. Forget that. Focus on what
you want out of life and go after it." Jen
waved a hand. "If we're done with Brian,
let's move on. I have news."

Her bright eyes darted over to Rebecca,
who smiled and clapped. Stephanie wondered whether she was the only one in the
room who didn't know…whatever it was…
because she'd launched into her dating woes.

As she finished her first cookie, Stephanie agreed. "Of course. You're right. I'm
being overdramatic. Men aren't the answer.
Living the life I want is. All I have to do is
figure out how." *And wait until everyone
who knows me has moved away so I don't
kill them with the shock of refusing to run
the Christmas parade or the back-to-school
supplies drive.*

Yates men and women were known for

their civic pride and unwavering service to Holly Heights. Admitting that she'd rather have a root canal than shovel up the road apples after the parade horses passed by would seem completely out of character. Bringing a rodeo clown to dinner might necessitate an intervention.

Jen patted her leg. "Cheer up. It's the last day of school. Got our lottery ticket right here. You were voted Favorite Teacher at Holly Heights for the third year in a row."

"No, I *tied* for Favorite Teacher. Again. How is that even possible? How can a vote like this turn into a tie for three years in a row?" She and Rebecca turned to Jen. "You're the math teacher. Got any idea how that might happen?"

"None. I'd suspect someone was tampering with the vote, but this is a popularity contest and not a real election." Jen smoothed her hair behind her ear as she stretched forward to pour wine into three glasses. "Haven't you won enough popularity contests—Class President, Best Dressed and Miss Congeniality? Even Rebecca, the most supportive person in history, is getting tired of clapping."

Rebecca was sending death glares at Jen, despite her Suzy Homemaker apron with its cheery sunflowers. But then Rebecca smiled sweetly and patted Stephanie's hand. "Ignore her. Jealousy. I'll clap for you until my hands fall off."

Jen snorted and they all three laughed. Stephanie had to admit Jen had a point. She could let this contest go. Tying was almost as good as winning.

Said the eternal best friend.

Even in her own mind she was the spunky sidekick instead of the star of the show.

"Switch places with me." Stephanie stood up and tugged Jen's hand.

"What? Why? This is my spot. I like my spot." Jen grumbled and moved over to sprawl on the couch. "Ugh. How uncomfortable."

Rebecca poked Jen. "Get a grip. A change in outlook could do you *both* some good."

Stephanie pretended to whistle innocently as Rebecca raised an eyebrow at her. The message was loud and clear.

Stephanie stared up at the unfamiliar patch

of ceiling over Jen's usual chair. Nothing was any clearer on this side of the room. "A good job, a nice family, the best friends in the world—why can't I be happy with that?" Most of the people in Holly Heights chose to live there because of its easy distance to Austin and the benefits of small-town community. Her mother was content. Even Jen and Rebecca were cheerfully anticipating the summer.

"You're bringing me down. We are officially on vacation, and this is going to be a summer like no other." Rebecca clapped her hands but stopped and fiddled with her apron when Jen gave her the warning look.

Jen slid their lottery ticket across the coffee table. "There's always next year for Favorite Teacher. Eventually Ms. Diaz will set aside her periodic table and retire so all you have to do is outlast her. Things are looking up for us." She picked up her wineglass and raised it. With her sleek haircut, layers of thrift-store chic, tall boots and the rakish tilt of her chin to accompany her raised glass, Jen was a cross between a fashion model and a swashbuckler prepared to take on the world.

Actually, the description fit Jen pretty well. "We need a toast." Jen waited patiently for the other two to raise their glasses. "To possibilities, taking chances and a long summer."

"And to friends who remind us what's important," Rebecca added.

"Vacation!" Stephanie said. They clinked glasses and each one took a sip of good wine.

Rebecca picked up the ticket and closed one eye to read the print. Did she need glasses? Yes. Would she wear them? No. "You changed the numbers."

"I did," Jen answered in a singsong voice. "I let the machine pick this time. Roll the dice. Trust the universe. Et cetera and so forth. What could it hurt?"

"Have you checked the winning numbers yet?" Stephanie shoved the seductive plate of cookies farther away while she wondered what was up with Jen. She never did a singsong anything.

"If we're winners, what will you spend your share on?" Jen crossed one long leg over the other. The secondhand boots she'd rescued looked fabulous on her bouncing foot. "Other than paying off student loans and buying a car with windows that completely roll up, which seems to be the height of my imagination." Jen closed her eyes and moaned as she bit into a cookie. "I'd definitely pay Rebecca to make these for me every single day."

"That would make it easier for me to give everything away. I could live in your guesthouse, clean your pool and make cookies every day. Sounds like a plan to me." Rebecca stretched her arms wide, her blond curls and blue eyes shining like that of the perfect animated princess. Stephanie was glad to know Rebecca had some of her own imperfections. They never would have been friends this long without them. "Imagine all the good millions could do."

Jen shook her head. "Even playing make-believe you have to save the world. It must be genetic." Stephanie's stomach knotted at the threat of changing the topic to Rebecca's brother, Daniel. She did not want to go there. She definitely would need more cookies if they did.

Rebecca held up a hand. "Well, how about this? I would buy myself a gourmet kitchen.

Cooking on my mother's old stove is nostalgic, but I wouldn't mind six burners. Ooh, and a commercial refrigerator, one with the deep freezer drawer." Stephanie and Jen exchanged a knowing look as Rebecca dreamed of appliances. "And granite countertops on a big island." The hushed tone she used suggested it was a life goal, not simply a practical upgrade.

Stephanie tried to guess how many times they'd sat in the same places through the years and discussed all the important issues. Rebecca's house had been their gathering spot as girls and nothing much had changed, even though her parents had retired and moved to a sunny beach and her brother was off saving the world one patient at a time. This place was home. It was easy to dream crazy dreams here.

Neither Jen nor Rebecca seemed to want to change that, even with the world of possibilities a lottery win could bring.

"You'd never leave this place," Jen said. "Be honest."

Stephanie stiffened but relaxed as she realized Jen was talking to Rebecca.

"No, but I would remodel it to within an inch of its life. Hire a handsome contractor, buy top-of-the-line everything and know I was the luckiest woman in the world. I love this place, but it could be upgraded." Rebecca picked up a cookie and waved it. "We all know the food's just as good now coming from my cramped out-of-date kitchen, but it sure would be fun to have expensive toys."

"Okay, so I'm paying off bills and hiring staff. Bex is giving it all away, either in the form of checks or to-go plates from her fancy kitchen. What are you going to do, Steph?" Jen asked.

"I would…" Her voice trailed off. Jen and Rebecca knew her better than anyone. Why was she afraid to be honest with them? For some reason it was hard to confess she wanted something else, something different than what she had. "I would travel. Go to Paris. See the Eiffel Tower and the Louvre and get out of Holly Heights for a while."

Jen pursed her lips. "I could see that. Be back in time to hand out the syllabus on the first day, but rack up some travel miles before that. Maybe, after all the bills were paid, I'd get a passport and join you."

Stephanie wasn't so sure she'd report back to work the first day of school if she had any other way to pay the bills. Lately, it seemed as if every day was the same.

"Would you come back?" Rebecca asked, the look in her eyes serious as she studied Stephanie's face. "To Holly Heights?"

"What? Of course she would. She practically runs the place, thanks to her forefathers and general popularity. How does she even have time to date, what with all the civic duty?" Jen propped her boots on the table. "Where else could you go to get the royal treatment?"

Nowhere. She couldn't go anywhere else in the world and find people who remembered her winning the spelling bee in fourth grade or her mother's prizewinning cherry pie or her grandfather's years of service as the county judge or how helpful she was or sweet or funny or…boring. Jen was right. She was popular in Holly Heights, but sometimes she wanted to try meeting people without her history waving behind her.

Likable was fine, but maybe she could be interesting somewhere else.

"The town would fall apart if the last Yates moved away." Jen sighed. "And so would we."

"No need to worry. This is home." And it was. Rebecca and Jen were family. The Yateses were big believers in family.

"Doesn't mean you can't see the world," Rebecca said. "You know, with your imaginary lottery winnings. You've planned a thousand trips with your collection of travel guides and coffee table books. The money could mean you stop planning and start going."

Sure. New, lucky, rich Stephanie could be adventurous. That would be interesting.

And if the freedom she'd been dreaming of didn't make her happy, she'd have to assume there was something wrong with her, not her hometown.

She needed to dream bigger.

"You're right. So, instead of taking a trip I've planned a million times, I'd put on a blindfold and throw a dart at the map. I'd aim for Paris, but how exciting would it be to pack a bag, get on a plane and go see someplace you've never thought of?" She leaned her head back and imagined herself deplaning from a private jet. Somehow she was dressed like Audrey Hepburn in *Breakfast at Tiffany's* because why not.

When she realized how quiet the other two had gotten, she opened her eyes to see them both watching her closely. "What?"

"You, go somewhere without careful planning, the required shots and an insurance policy against acts of God? That sounds wrong." Jen stood up, topped off the wineglasses and added, "But I like it. Let's do it."

Annoyed all over again at how impossible it was to try something new without everyone reminding her that it was out of character, Stephanie said, "Do what? Just…win the lottery?"

"I'm pretty sure the darts are still in Daniel's closet. We need a map." Rebecca stood up, shook out the skirt of her sundress and disappeared down the hallway.

Jen walked into the kitchen and came back with a dish towel. "Not a real blindfold but it should work. No peeking." She paused in front of Stephanie, grabbed her hand and started to pull her off the couch. "We'll go ahead with the dart in case we win and you need to jump on a plane quickly. You like to be prepared."

Giving in to Jen's demands, Stephanie eased up off the couch and smoothed down her Holly Heights High School T-shirt over her hips. "You act like you don't trust me." She yanked on her ponytail to tighten it and then waved her hands. "Wait, you act like we're actually going to win the lottery." Either one was a crazy thought.

Rebecca trotted back into the living room with a giant map poster and a dart. "I'm not sure all these countries still exist, but Paris should be there." She yanked open a closet door and taped up the poster. "Remember when we had a dartboard here? Daniel smoked us every time we played."

Stephanie crossed her arms over her chest and said nothing. She didn't have to. Jen and Rebecca both turned to stare at her.

"I got an email from him yesterday. Sounds like things are going well," Rebecca said and studied her carefully. "And then there are his Facebook updates." Rebecca raised her eyebrows and dared Stephanie to say she had no idea what she was talking about.

The thing about best friends is that they never forget your first love or first crush or whatever it was she'd had for Daniel Lincoln, her best friend's older brother and the first male to shove her into the role of friend when she'd wanted more. Bravely asking him to dinner had been an un-Stephanie kind of thing to do. Doing it on his worst day ever was poor planning.

Nobody had forgotten it, actually. But that whole fiasco had happened a long time ago. Now he wasn't even in Holly Heights, and her friends had already established she could never leave because the town would fold without her.

The risk she'd taken in telling him how she felt hadn't paid off. His easy rejection had made it clear he'd never seen her as anything other than an adopted little sister.

That didn't mean she'd made a mistake or that stepping out on a limb this time would mean failure. If she never made a change, she'd never know what was possible.

"Give me the blindfold. I'm ready to hop on a plane to anywhere, you wait and see." She tied the dish towel over her eyes and held out her hand. Jen pressed the dart into her palm and said, "See the map. Be the map." They all chuckled, remembering countless slumber parties where Daniel had tried to show them how to hit the dartboard instead of the innocent closet door.

Rebecca put her hands on Stephanie's shoulders and spun her around once. "Do your best!"

"Come on, Paris!" Her heart racing with excitement and fear, Stephanie tossed the dart and hoped to hit land. She could see herself stepping off a plane. Floating on a boat, not so much.

She tried to yank off the dish towel but Jen shoved her glass of wine in her hand. "Before you see where you're landing, let's make another toast. To new beginnings and lottery winnings."

Thinking they were spending a whole lot of time making plans for something that would never happen, Stephanie held out her glass, waited for the clink and took a sip. Then Jen yanked off her makeshift blindfold and said in her best game show host voice, "Let's see where you're headed."

The three of them lined up in front of the map. Somehow she'd completely missed France, not to mention the tiny dot of Paris. In fact, she'd overshot Europe as well. The dart was planted squarely in the middle of nowhere Peru.

"That's impossible. There's no way I missed the entire continent of Europe." The images of Peru that came to mind were of llamas and Machu Picchu, which she might enjoy seeing, but that was not where the dart had landed. No, apparently she was going to… Alto, a place she'd heard of once in her life thanks to a posting on Daniel Lincoln's Facebook page. She narrowed her eyes at Rebecca. "What did you do?"

"Have another cookie," Rebecca said and blinked her eyelashes as she held out the plate. Of the three of them, Rebecca had always been able to put on the best innocent face.

"I have no clue what you mean." Jen yanked down the map, folded it and handed the dart to Rebecca. "It seems your first destination is the Andes. When we win."

Stephanie wagged her finger at Rebecca. "You moved the dart. You had to. There's no way that I, the dart queen of 2001, would have missed by that much."

"Now why would I do that?" Rebecca asked.

Thanks to years of experience, Stephanie was skeptical of her perfectly angelic expression.

Rebecca narrowed her eyes at Jen. "Did you see me move the dart?"

"I did not." Jen shook her head firmly. Her boots shifted on the hardwood. "And for what reason would Rebecca send you to the area where her brother is working? I mean, what could she hope to gain from it? Have another cookie. You'll feel better."

Stephanie studied the plate of cookies Rebecca was waving under her nose. She crossed her arms again. "It doesn't matter. We won't win. I don't know why you'd… What? Push me in his direction. If you'll recall, I tried that once. He patted me on the head and told me he liked me too much to try dating. Remember? And he could *never* kiss me." She wrinkled her nose in the same way Daniel had when he'd said the word as if she'd asked him to *kiss* the south end of a north-bound donkey.

"People change, Steph. Maybe he has, too. He's lost his job, moved halfway around the world. That's got to cause some careful consideration of what's important in life." Jen turned to Rebecca. "He's not dating anyone, is he? Not that it matters."

"No, he's not dating. And getting involved with a man like Daniel would be a terrible idea. He's married to his job. But…" Rebecca shrugged.

When Rebecca didn't add anything else, Jen dropped back into her usual spot and kicked one jean-clad leg over the arm of the chair. "It's not like running into the guy you measure other guys against is a bad thing, is it? Maybe that's all you need to get out of the friend rut and on to the road to love, happiness and Favorite Teacher. Well, that and a few million dollars."

At the reminder of the nonexistent money needed to fuel this imaginary trip, Stephanie eased back against the couch again. They could tease her all they wanted. Nothing would come of it unless the numbers the machine had spit out were winners. She'd ask the math wizard in the group what the odds were, but she didn't want to let them know how shaken she was at the idea of either a trip to Peru or seeing Daniel Lincoln again in his no doubt trailblazing glory.

If she needed a mentor in learning to make new paths instead of waiting for things to change, he would be a solid choice.

As far as either of them knew, she'd had a crush and now it was over. Right? She watched Rebecca, her best friend since first grade, finish her cookie with what seemed to be a touch of smugness.

Then Rebecca and Jen glanced at each other and the smugness bloomed and spread.

Faking a stop in the Andes Mountains couldn't be that hard. She took a deep breath. Lying might not be the most honorable solution, but it would definitely be the easiest, and she wouldn't feel the least guilty about cheating a couple of dart-moving cheaters.

"We're going to hold you to your fabulous idea, Steph. One dart and you pack your bags, get on a plane. Unless you bring back photographic evidence of you, Daniel and his clinic in Alto, we're going to know you chickened out, you big chickeny chicken." Jen's satisfaction was hard to face, but Stephanie did her best not to show her dismay.

Rebecca wagged a finger. "Great idea, Jen. Evidence."

Stephanie snorted. "So what happens if I decide to take my millions and head for France and ignore the clucking sounds you make every time you see me from now until the end of time?"

"No cookies for you." Rebecca moved the plate out of reach and Jen whistled.

"Harsh but effective." Jen raised an eyebrow. "Not that you need consequences. You want to make a change. Here's the push you need. After we win the lottery."

"Okay, so you managed to fix the dart-throwing exhibition. If you can figure out a way to rig the lottery, I am going to be so impressed."

Jen exchanged a glance with Rebecca, and as soon as Stephanie put the wineglass on the table, Jen shouted, "We won!" She and Rebecca jumped up and down like the excitement could no longer be contained. "Five million dollars split three ways. We won!"

"Pack your bags," Rebecca sang as she hugged Stephanie. "It's time to make a wish come true."

Stephanie tipped her head to the side and raised an eyebrow. "You're talking about seeing Peru, right?"

"Sure." Rebecca blinked slowly. "What else could I be talking about?"

"Fine, but you're going with me," Stephanie muttered. And added through gritted teeth, "My treat." If she was going, she was certainly going to take a buffer with her.

"Can't." Rebecca held up her hand and ticked off the points. "No passport. No tranquilizers. No airplanes. No way." Her fear of flying was well documented. They'd tried it the first summer after her parents moved to Florida.

It had gone badly. Very badly. Now they took road trips.

"And Jen's out. She signed up to teach summer school."

Before Stephanie could argue that Jen had no need to pick up the extra money, Rebecca added, "This is your thing. You don't need us."

Oh, yes, she did. It was fine to dream big on Rebecca's sofa. Actually going to a foreign country all alone might be too big.

And the fact that she was sitting on the edge of panic over the trip instead of dancing in celebration over winning the lottery was something to think about. Later.

"Are you matchmaking?" Stephanie asked. "Because…"

"I love you. I love him. The two of you together, I don't know about, but you're in a rut. This ought to fix that." Rebecca wrapped her arm around Stephanie's shoulders. "And if I know my brother, his rut's deeper than yours, even on a mountaintop. Of the three of us, you were always the best at getting him to do what we wanted."

"But what do we want him to do?" There had to be an ironclad excuse to get out of this.

"Simple. I want him to be happy." Rebecca shrugged. "And you, too. What if the best way to stop turning dates into friends is to make a friend...something more? I dare you to give this a shot. One trip. Easy."

Stephanie was speechless as she considered Rebecca, who had walked away to pull a casserole out of the oven that was now living on borrowed time. Rebecca was her best friend. They would be friends until the end of time. But she might have been breathing in the oven fumes for too long.

Still, she could go, see Daniel and return with the message that he was happily saving the world one vaccination at a time. The trip also would prove that her feelings had been settled, once and for all. He was a friend. He'd stay a friend.

And having a purpose made the trip a little less intimidating.

But only a little.

Ready or not, she was headed for Peru.

CHAPTER TWO

"WHY ARE YOU updating now, you stupid piece of junk?" Daniel rubbed his forehead, watched his laptop count up slowly and tried to think happy thoughts. Before he'd settled in to start and finish the overdue fund-raising report, he'd checked his parents' Facebook page. The cruise to Alaska was going well. But there were no other updates. Nothing from his sister. He would've called her to check in, but his recent uptick in homesickness wouldn't be helped by hearing her voice.

Since he'd been about half a second away from hitting the medical recruiting sites he'd started checking now and then, just to see who was hiring close to home, he should thank his computer for saving him the angst.

While giving him a whole different bucket of angst, of course.

His life was in Peru. He missed home and

his sister more than he'd ever admit, but he was a grown man. He'd deal. There was plenty to do here to keep his mind off what he was missing in Holly Heights.

Daniel scanned the small lobby restaurant and watched three guys in business suits working happily on laptops with better timing than his. At least he wasn't trying to do this in a necktie and white coat. The doctor's dress code had been replaced with comfortable jeans, his favorite Baylor T-shirt and a dusty ball cap that kept the sun out of his eyes.

Most of the time, he was the lone doctor in town. He had the freedom to dress the way he wanted and run the best clinics he could.

That had to be the unlikely silver lining to his flameout at Holly Heights Hospital. Refusing to discharge a patient whose insurance wasn't up to par—against his sound judgment as a doctor—was one thing. Insulting the hospital administrator in front of the board was where he'd stepped over the line. And as a result the hospital's summer job shadowing program for high school kids—the one his sister had drafted and he'd called in every single favor he could to get approved—had also been axed.

Letting Rebecca down had been a hard way to learn the lesson, but he'd never again make the mistake of believing his skills made him bulletproof. Even worse was imagining the disappointed kids who might have missed out on finding their calling.

In Peru he didn't have to worry about offending any number crunchers in expensive suits. Well, except for the guy watching him over the top of his newspaper.

Daniel shoved the computer out of the way, yanked his breakfast plate closer and scooped up a heaping tower of fluffy scrambled eggs. At least this meal was on his schedule. That was one of the perks of this business-class hotel in Lima. Everything ran on time. Reliable electricity. Running water twenty-four hours a day. And hot water whenever he turned on the tap. City life definitely had its bonuses.

When the laptop finally whirred back on, he sighed and reopened the document he'd been staring at for long minutes before his computer had taken its life in its hands by shutting down and restarting without his permission.

He smiled at the woman who kept his coffee cup full. After she'd gone, he ate his toast and tried to come up with the next paragraph of his fund-raising report for HealthyAmericas.

The patterns on the ceiling hadn't changed since the last time he'd stared up for inspiration. "I should have found someone else to work on this report." Not that he'd really trust anyone else with something so important. He was the project leader. The success or failure of HealthyAmericas outreach in the Pasco region rested squarely on his shoulders.

"And success depends pretty heavily on money, so you shouldn't have put this off, idiot." He surveyed the room to see the other diners shooting glances at him out of the corners of their eyes and decided talking to himself was a habit better left to long hikes in the Andes Mountains. Apparently it made the city people nervous.

"The clinic in Alto continues to serve the population of the town and the surrounding

region through vaccinations and basic…"
Boring. Why would anyone care about these
colorful, three-dimensional people when all
he could give them was gray, flat statistics?
"I could write a report about one patient,
make it clear how donations help an indi-
vidual. People love to hear feel-good stories.
Especially about cute kids."

The businessman seated across from him
wrinkled his nose as though he wasn't quite
convinced, and the idea of starting all over
again made Daniel want to escape. Head
back to the mountains. Get his hands dirty
and make a difference the best way he knew
how.

But coughs needed medication, cuts needed
stitches, and there were babies and mothers
and little ladies with arthritic hands or worse
all depending on this funding.

Why did good medicine always seem to
come down to money?

When his email dinged, he seized his chance
to do anything else and clicked to open the
message from his sister.

"Won the lottery?" Daniel laughed out
loud in relief. His sister would write a check,

no problem. "And Jen and Steph, too." His fist pump froze all activity in the restaurant while everyone waited to see what the crazy American would do next. He waved his arms broadly. "Good news!"

They all smiled awkwardly in return and kept on watching him surreptitiously.

He went back to the message and reread it. "A big investor coming here? Today? I don't have time for that." He tried to imagine what sort of businessperson would come all the way to Lima to check out his operation and decided it didn't matter. He needed donations.

The plate of scrambled eggs and toast was demolished in a flurry of happy bites before he fired off a congratulatory email with the standard "make a donation now" request. Then he quickly drafted another message for Dr. Wright, a medical school colleague who'd founded HealthyAmericas, to let her know big donations were on the way and that his fund-raising letter would be delayed but he'd have it ready for the big donor event in two months.

"Or else," Daniel muttered. He added

his regrets that he couldn't make it back to Texas in time for the event before he hit Send. She wanted him to be the face of the doctors serving in South America. He was pretty sure he didn't want to show his face around there. Too many people would remember him leaving in disgrace. Austin was close to Holly Heights and it was a small, small world.

He clasped his hands behind his head, stretched in his chair and studied the ceiling again. "Definitely a case study. Maybe a few, with pictures to show the real-life benefits of having medical teams making regular stops. That's the way to go." He ignored the curious stares and tried to think of someone who could do a good job with the report in order to free up his time for more patients. "I should request an intern or something, somebody who's good with a camera and a computer."

Making a mental note to add that to his budget for the next year, he closed the laptop, shoved it in the beat-up bag he carried with him at all times and pulled out his wallet to leave *nuevo soles* as a tip. He smiled at the waitress again. "*Gracias.*"

Before he could head back to Alto, he had to check out of the hotel and make sure the truck with the medical supplies was scheduled to deliver next week. And now he needed to come back to the hotel to meet with this investor. Flights arrived early from the States, so he should still be able to make it to Alto. He'd leave a message at the desk with a time and hope whoever it was checked in soon.

Every day he had a long list of things to do, so he was glad to push off the report that was making him crazy. When he made it back to Lima in another two weeks, he'd do it. Definitely.

A husky laugh drew his attention to the lobby desk where Paulo was talking with a tall blonde dressed for African safari. She was khakied and cargoed from head to toe, although silky hair trailed down her back. Something about her was familiar, but that could be attributed to the homesickness that struck now and then. He was happy in Peru, but that didn't mean he never dreamed of going back to the way things were, when he was such a skilled surgeon he could bend the rules as he liked. As always, he shoved aside the disappointment and stood as the blonde turned away from the desk.

"Stephanie?" He had to sit back down before his weak knees made him stumble.

Stephanie pulled out the chair opposite him, but before she sat down, she wrapped her arms around his neck and squeezed so tight he almost turned blue. The hug surprised him, but it shouldn't have. She'd always greeted him the same way. The bigger shock was that he wasn't quite ready to let her go when she braced both hands against his chest. She smelled like lavender dryer sheets and about a million things he'd learned not to take for granted, things that made him think of home.

And immediately he was reminded of how sweet she'd been when she'd asked him out to dinner. Since he'd just burned every bridge at the hospital, he hadn't been as careful with her as he should have been. Protecting Rebecca, Stephanie and Jen had been his job ever since the first night he'd been stuck babysitting.

Seeing her here brought his homesickness back—with a crash. He'd missed her. She was home and family and laughing and not taking himself so seriously in one beautiful, sweet package. He realized he was still holding on to her hands and forced himself to let go.

"What are you doing here?" He frowned as she settled in the chair with a tired sigh.

"The frown's more like it. For half a second I thought you were happy to see me." She rolled her eyes at him and waved the waitress over.

"Yes, ma'am, what would you like to order? May I bring you a menu?"

Stephanie waved her hands. "No, no need for that much trouble. How about eggs and toast? Orange juice?"

The waitress wrote down her order. "Certainly. I'll have that right out."

Stephanie clapped her hands. "Wonderful." Before the waitress could walk off, she added, "Before you go, those are great shoes. Are they comfortable?"

Daniel did his best to keep the annoyance at a low simmer while the two women discussed comfortable shoes and where to find them in Lima. By the time the waitress walked off he was amazed she and Stephanie hadn't exchanged phone numbers.

"So you're surprised to see me. Didn't Rebecca let you know I was coming?" Stephanie's gaze darted away. "I'm happy to see you, too, by the way."

The discomfort on her face reminded him that even if he'd almost forgotten their last awkward conversation, maybe she hadn't. He hated that. He didn't want anything to change between them. That had been the whole point of turning her down. Stephanie had always looked up to him. He'd watched over her. That was the arrangement he was comfortable with.

"No, she didn't mention it. Obviously. You nearly missed me. I was about to go pick up medical supplies." And now he had no idea what to do. Time to prepare would have been nice. "Did you buy one of everything at Camping Corral?"

She frowned at her outfit, studied his for

a long minute and then grimaced. "Okay, I overdid it. A little. But this is what happens without enough time to study a place."

As she surveyed the lobby, she pointed at the skylight. "Clouds. That's something I didn't expect. I had this picture of sunshine and green mountains, not oceans and heavy cloud cover."

"You can get that here, too. Wait an hour and everything changes." He watched her lean back and thank the waitress with a friendly smile.

"How wonderful. Scrambled eggs are my favorite. They're the perfect start for a beautiful day. I bet you hear that all the time, don't you?" She picked up a fork and waited patiently for the waitress's answer.

The woman stopped and thought for a minute. "No, ma'am, I don't. But I like a good breakfast, so it's nice to meet another fan." She pointed at the skylight. "And it's nice to meet someone else who isn't bothered by a few clouds."

Of course she wasn't bothered by clouds. Stephanie was like sunshine—wherever she went it was only a matter of time until the clouds passed.

The waitress made sure to pour Stephanie a nice cup of coffee. She happily dug into her breakfast and he shook his head as the waitress brought her a fresh bowl of jelly, a stack of clean napkins and a paper from the front desk.

He'd had to lay down a healthy tip to get service with the same friendly attitude.

"I'm sure you're in a hurry to get on with whatever brings you to Peru." He was always in a hurry. He sipped his lukewarm coffee and wondered if he could get her to ask for a refill. "How long are you here?" *And could you just hand me the checks and let me get back to my day?*

The homesickness had no cure, but getting back to work would help the symptoms.

She fiddled with the edge of the folded napkins for a minute and the niggling thought that everything wasn't going to go according to his plan settled in his brain.

"Your sister, Jen and I have this sort of agreement. Maybe it's a dare. I'm not really sure." She picked up a slice of toast and carefully, thoughtfully chewed it all while he did his best to ignore the impatience he could feel building with the tick of the clock. He rested his elbows on the table, propped his chin on his hands and pretended he was patient.

"I threw a dart. It landed on Alto. I have to go there or listen to them clucking at me for the rest of my life." She shrugged. "You get that, right?"

He leaned back in his chair and wondered who in the world could figure out what was happening from a nonsensical statement like that.

Only one who'd spent countless Friday nights listening to his sister and her friends giggle over badly thrown darts. He'd also learned to carefully consider every sentence that came out of Stephanie's mouth. She'd always been the one to give him the most trouble. Rebecca he could threaten into compliance by mentioning their parents. He was pretty sure nothing threatened Jen but she'd never tried cajoling him, either. All that had come from Stephanie. At sixteen she'd been good at getting cooperation, even from a cocky high school senior.

"Let me translate. You won the lottery. They dared you to throw a dart at the map and get on a plane. If you don't do it, they'll never let you forget it." And just like when they were kids, he'd been dragged into their brilliant plan.

The urge to lecture her on the dangers of traveling alone to spots off the beaten path was strong.

"Sort of. You've got the basics anyway." She spread grape jelly on her toast. "So, how soon can we leave for Alto? I need a picture of you, me and your clinic. Then I'll be out of your hair and you'll have some nice donations."

She didn't meet his gaze as she said it, so he was pretty sure that wasn't the full story. "You want to come to Alto?" He shook his head. "Impossible."

"There's the reaction I was expecting," she muttered and sipped her steaming hot coffee.

"Now the safari getup makes more sense, but—" he yanked off his ball cap and ruffled his hand through the hair that was long enough to drive him crazy, something he didn't need with a woman bound to get him there in two seconds flat "—it's a hard drive and once you get there the amenities are seriously lacking. The Andes can be dangerous, and if you fall or break something, it's a long, painful ride back to Lima. It's nothing like home. Better just leave the check. If you're determined to see the sights, head to the tourist towns or even stay here for a few days. It's a nice place. Lots of interesting history. The hot running water will be right up your alley."

If he warned her about the traffic, protecting her valuables and being aware of her surroundings, Stephanie would mock him. He might deserve it. The dangers in Lima were much the same as in any big city and she'd been navigating Houston and Austin with two troublemakers at her side for years.

Stephanie pursed her lips and pushed away her empty plate. Instead of dragging in like a woman who'd spent most of the night on a plane, she seemed energetic. Full of life. She always had.

"Here's the thing. We can do this the easy way or the hard way, but I've flown halfway around the world to satisfy the doubters back home, have a little adventure and, yes, leave you a big check." Stephanie shook her head. "The question you have to ask yourself is how bad you want it. Bad enough to play tour guide for a couple of days?"

"I moved to Peru to avoid donor *requests* like this, Stephanie. You know I have important work to do. The drive up to Alto takes a full day, but there are stops to make along the way because there are people who need doctors, don't have them and have no way to get to them. So I go to them. I'm too busy for a sightseeing trip." He banged his hand against his bag. "By the time I make it to Alto, unload the medical supplies, hike out to all the villages that need attention and come back to Lima, you're looking at two weeks. Nobody has time to load you up and bring you back to wash your hair."

She blinked as though he'd slapped her, and Daniel noticed the guy with the paper had pursed his lips and was shaking his head in disapproval. Daniel sighed. The nosy guy was right. She didn't know how hard the travel was and treating her like some shallow nuisance was unfair. Besides, he didn't like the way disappointing her made him feel.

"Sorry. That was a little more forceful than I'd intended." He spread his hand out over the cursed laptop. "I have a few things on my mind."

"No 'Hi, how've you been?' or even 'What's new?' or 'What brings you to the neighborhood?' Just full-on skipping the small talk and telling me how busy you are." She nodded. "At least you haven't changed much."

"Did you hope I would? Change?" The question about whether she thought time in the mountains would make him think differently of her and their…romantic potential hovered on the tip of his tongue, but he wouldn't ask it. He was afraid of her answer. Friends were a lot more valuable and harder to come by than dates. Or at least he thought that was still true.

"Not really, no, although you *could* stand to relax." She raised her eyebrows at him and just like that he could picture her teasing him in front of the dartboard. Even in high school he'd been driven. His sister and her friends had sort of adopted him, included him and teased him for the arrogance that had raged nearly unchecked until he'd hit medical school and someone educated it out of him.

She patted his hand as though she was consoling an ailing relative, and he realized his own lofty opinion of his importance still didn't mean much to her.

"Don't you remember that time you ran out of gas down by Sarah Anderson's house? We *borrowed* your dad's car and rescued you. Who kept your secret? Who made sure no one knew the infallible Daniel Lincoln did something as everyday human as running out of gas while driving past a pretty girl's house? I did. If you want to ease up on telling me how important you are, I'll make sure I keep that secret, too." She tugged his bag out from under his hand. "What's so valuable in here? You've got a death grip on it."

"You can't go, Steph. There's no room for you in my schedule." He hated to say it so baldly, but the truth was always the best choice. "I need your donations. Money like this will accomplish so much, but I have work to do."

She ignored him. Of course. After she flipped open the bag and saw a laptop, she shut it again and pouted a little. "I was hoping for something to use as blackmail. Of course you were working. You're always working."

"How do you know? We haven't seen each other in years." He didn't like the idea that he couldn't surprise her.

"You told me you hadn't changed, D. You would never lie." Her eyes weren't quite as reserved this time when he managed to catch her attention.

The connection that stretched between them was sweet and made him uneasy at the same time. He needed her friendship. Anything else was dangerous. Besides, she was like a sister. They'd already survived acne, cafeteria pizza and countless fights over the remote. There was no way romance could outlast that.

"Listen, I'm happy to see you, but coming to Alto is a bad plan. The conditions aren't what you're used to and—"

"And you're afraid I'll tumble right on into love with you again. It's okay. I'm smarter now than I was then. I realized you were right. We are good friends, but that doesn't mean we should be anything more. Don't worry." She squeezed his hand. "Friends. That's all. Now help me show your sister and Jen that they don't know everything they think they do. Take me to Alto. I'll stay until you're coming back to Lima. I might even be able to help."

"You aren't a doctor. You'll slow me down." He closed his eyes against her wince. "I've got a group waiting, and I need to focus. We'll be hiking and setting up clinics during the day and at night, I've got to work on this fund-raising report to keep the doors open. It's a lot, Steph. Can't you just..."

"Write a check? Make you happy? Get out of your way?" Stephanie reached for the backpack she'd set down next to her chair. She pulled out a digital camera and a nice leather-bound journal. "For my travel blog. The one I'm going to write. For me. I won the lottery. I'm going to travel and I'm going to document it all." She tapped her finger on top of the journal and watched him while she waited for his brain to work everything out.

"You could help me. Instead of an annoying intern—"

"You could have an annoying donor with a large, healthy checkbook whose single wish is to see Alto and help you with your fundraising. Just imagine…killing two birds with one trip. That has to please the always busy Dr. Lincoln even if Daniel is remembering my unfortunate habit of singing pop tunes at the top of my lungs."

"They're all in Spanish here," he said, frowning. She had a point. She also had the equipment, and an English teacher should be able to craft something people would enjoy reading. HealthyAmericas would benefit from the trip. He could use the help.

"Once I hear them a few times, I'm sure I can mangle the Spanish cheerfully." Stephanie raised the camera and snapped a quick photo of him.

"Intense concentration. Wonder how many shots it would take to get any other expression?" she asked as she flipped through the shots on her camera.

"Two weeks and you'll write me a check for twenty-five thousand dollars. Plus, you'll help me draft a compelling report to help HealthyAmericas with the upcoming donor event." He offered her his hand.

Stephanie studied it closely. "How about a check for twice that and two more from some dear friends? And I'll make sure I'm more help than hindrance on this trip." Then she held out her hand.

"You're really bad at negotiation. You went the wrong direction. Yes to the checks, but stick to the report, please. That'll be a big weight off my shoulders." He waved his hand impatiently.

She slipped her hand in his and the warm shock of soft skin and awareness surprised him. He squeezed her hand and then nodded.

"Come on. Don't look so serious. We're going to have fun. You'll see." When she straightened up, pulling her hand away, he had the impression that he missed her hand in his. After a second's touch. Crazy.

Had to be the homesickness. That's all.

"Two rules before we go." He tightened his hand in a fist under the table and waited.

Stephanie crossed her arms over her chest with a gusty sigh. "How did I know there was more negotiation coming? Did you think I needed the practice?"

"I don't want to talk about Holly Heights Hospital. At all." He waited for her to agree, watched her open her mouth to argue and then reluctantly close it.

"Fine. But you need to talk to someone. It's been four years. It's only a big thing in your own mind, and your sister wants…" She shook her head. "What's the second rule?"

He was glad she'd stopped. He and Rebecca had always been close and missing her made it harder to be happy doing this job that mattered so much. He wasn't sure what he'd do if Rebecca asked him to come home to Texas.

Focus. She hasn't asked and you have a job to do, visitors from home or not.

"You're going to have to follow my orders. My trip means my rules."

"Bossy. Just like old times." Stephanie rolled her eyes. "I'll try. That's all I can promise. I never graduated from obedience training, Doc."

This would be a disaster. One way or another, she'd interfere with his work. But he wanted the help and having a piece of home so close was hard to resist.

He turned his wrist over to check the time and then reviewed everything he still had to get done before they could leave Lima. "How much luggage do you have?"

Stephanie jerked in her seat as though she hadn't quite believed he'd give in. He should have negotiated harder. He tried to remember how many times he'd ever won against Stephanie and decided he'd never stood a chance anyway. She pointed over her shoulder. "See the pile next to the desk? That's all mine."

From here he could count two big suitcases and three duffle bags. "More khaki?"

She tapped her lips with one finger. "Are you making a joke? It's so hard to tell."

"There's no way we're dragging all that with us. Go through and cull to one bag. Make good choices. Pants, shirts, things we can wash if we have to." He checked under the table and nearly winced. "Unless you've worn those hiking boots for more than the plane ride down here, bring along your running shoes. And Band-Aids. Sunscreen. I'll be back in two hours. I'll tell Paulo to store the rest of your bags with mine so you can pick them up on your way home." He scooted back from the table and stood, ready to execute his plan.

Until Stephanie held up one soft hand and said, "Wait a minute. I respectfully request a question-and-answer period with each sweeping order, sir."

"Two rules. You can't keep up with two?" He sighed. "I knew this was a terrible plan."

Her lip twitched. "But you still want my money."

"I do." He tapped his left foot impatiently.

"And my help?" She batted her eyelashes at him and he could remember so many other times when she'd been able to tease him out of whatever cloud he'd been under.

"I do." She wouldn't back out now, would she?

"Fine. My backpack is okay, right? It's got all my camera stuff." She shoved her camera and journal in and stood while she waited for his answer.

"Yes. One bag and your backpack." Some of the tension in his neck and shoulders that had been building into a low-level headache eased when she saluted and clicked the rubber soles of her boots.

"I'll meet you right here. Should we synchronize our watches?" She held up her bare, slender wrist and tapped it as if she was trying to get a stopped watch working again.

He was shaking his head when he grabbed his bag and walked off, but there was something exciting about facing the trip he'd already made so many times with a new partner. Whether she disliked the journey or actively hated it, she'd be a lot of fun along the way. Stephanie Yates made sure everyone enjoyed life if it was possible. That was why the town of Holly Heights had loved her since she sprang into the world with a dimple and a bow taped to her head. He'd seen the pictures. She was adorable. And that was why the waitress hugged her neck on the way out.

"Miss Yates is going to leave her bags here while we make the run to Alto." He slid some money across the desk. "She'll need a room to rest and repack, but we'll be leaving this afternoon."

"Certainly, Doctor. I'll be more than happy

to help," Paulo answered as he slid the nuevo soles into his back pocket.

Daniel paused in the doorway to watch Paulo scramble to lift what had to be enough luggage for three months. As Paulo led Stephanie to the elevator, she turned and waved, looking like an adventurous ray of sunshine in the light streaming down from the skylight.

He didn't know whether to thank his sister for sending him a slice of home or to curse her. Life on the mountain was hard enough. Once he got used to laughing with Stephanie Yates, he was afraid he'd see the hard work that much more clearly.

Not that it mattered. Hard work was nothing. He was helping people, and that was all he'd ever wanted to do. Coming here had been hard, but now he'd found what he'd spent his life preparing for. Sometimes he wished things were different, that he was back home or just…not alone.

He didn't need distractions.

If anything was guaranteed, it was that Stephanie Yates would be a fun, frustrating, beautiful distraction. And to be honest, he was sort of looking forward to it.

CHAPTER THREE

STEPHANIE MADE SURE to arrive fifteen minutes early because she knew Daniel would be there ten minutes before the agreed upon time. Since he'd had to chauffer them around more than once before she got her first car, she, Rebecca, and Jen had often heard his opinion on the rudeness of keeping other people waiting. Even in high school he'd been attached to his schedule.

And if she'd spent one more minute in the comfortable hotel room, she might have decided Daniel was right. She'd called her mother to say she'd arrived safely, and her mom's long list of the threats she should be prepared for had worn her down. How her mother had any concept of the dangers, Stephanie wasn't sure. She hadn't left Texas. Ever.

But the warnings turned up the heat under the anxiety she'd tried to hide from Daniel.

She could give him a check and do some sightseeing here in the comfort of the big city before hopping on a plane back to her safe small town.

Playing it safe was smart. Comfortable. Easy. But in this case it would also mean failure.

Convincing him to go along with her plan had been a long shot.

Now she had to follow through, even if the idea of heading off into the unknown was giving her Texas-sized butterflies in her stomach. Daniel would keep her safe. All she had to do was keep her emotions in line.

Stephanie was casually filing her nails when Daniel strode through the open door. She nearly grinned at his slightly disgruntled frown when he spotted her. Victory.

"Have you been waiting long?" he asked. "Nobody will notice your manicure in Alto."

"Multitasking." She waved a hand. "You know how I hate to waste time."

He studied her face, and Stephanie tried to fight the warm flush headed straight to her cheeks. Daniel had always been good at calling her bluff.

"Or maybe you aren't as excited about this trip now that you've had some time to think on it." He paused, one hand over the handle of her suitcase.

He was giving her another chance to back out, which made pretending she didn't want to twice as hard, but she was committed. "Nope. I'm all in." Petrified, but committed.

When he didn't even grunt or grimace at the strain of carrying a bag that she'd dragged, with two rest stops, to the lobby, Stephanie decided that living in the Andes had built up his muscles. Watching them flex in his arms as he tossed the bag in the back of the pickup truck confirmed this suspicion. Also, it was fun.

"I haven't been down here for long, but I wouldn't dare keep you waiting," she said as she slid into the passenger seat and slammed the door. After efficiently buckling her seatbelt, she cleared her throat. "I remember how well you wait. And we both know you would've grabbed the first chance to leave me behind, like you left your sister and me at home that time we insisted on going to the movies with you."

This time he grunted as he stuck the key in the ignition and started the truck. "How long does it take to put on a pair of jeans?"

"For teenage girls? Eternity. Not any pair will do." Stephanie studied her cargo pants. She should have spent more time on her own wardrobe.

The windshield was already covered with enough insects to be bulletproof, but the interior of the truck was spotless. Just as she'd expect. Determined to be so quiet Daniel wouldn't even know she was there, she watched the beaches whiz by as they sped down the highway. She didn't remark on how the mountains ended so abruptly at rocky beaches and crashing waves or the guy riding a ten-speed down the side of the highway or the men selling fruit out of the trunks of cars or the boxes lining the hillside that were obviously homes. And she definitely didn't ask what the speed limit was. That took real courage. When she noticed how white her knuckles were, she painfully unwrapped her hand from the door and stretched her fingers.

Finally Daniel pulled over at a gas station

and turned off the engine. "Better go in and stock up on all the necessities. From here we turn off the paved road. No gas stations. Restrooms are harder to come by. Next stop is about forty miles."

Thinking that wouldn't take long at the speed of light or whatever the speed limit was, she answered, "I can wait."

He shook his head. "No. Go. Now. That forty miles could take the rest of the afternoon. Besides, I warned you about the restrooms. They're less reliable until we reach Alto."

Deciding he'd be difficult to live with if she ignored his instructions and he was right—and realizing she'd be crazy to turn her back on time to shop—she slid out of the truck, watched him unload a few gas cans and headed for the station.

"*Hola*," she called out as the bells jangled on the slamming door. The young woman behind the counter waved. Stephanie thought about asking where the restrooms were in Spanish, one of the few phrases she remembered, but the sign was hard to miss. And it was in English.

She made use of the facilities and then decided to get a drink for the road. Instead of an overwhelming supply of choices she didn't recognize, her favorite red-and-white can made for an easy decision. With three cold bottles in the basket she found by the door, Stephanie added what seemed to be plain potato chips and a big bag of individually wrapped chocolates. Chocolate was always a good idea. Frowning as she considered what might happen in the sunshine, she added another bag of hard candy. Too much candy was never a problem.

"Playing it safe already?" Daniel asked as he pulled open the glass door and pulled out two bottles filled with some kind of yellow drink.

"I thought those were your orders. We're turning off the paved road, leaving the world as I know it behind, so I should cling to the familiar while I can." She tightened her grip on the basket. "Besides, I like Coke and chips."

He tapped a bottle. "You'll like this, too. Inca Kola. It's like Peruvian Coke."

"But I already have Peruvian Coke. I mean,

it's actually Coke." She trailed behind him on the way to the cash register and watched him discuss what she thought was the weather with the woman behind the counter while he unloaded her basket. Everything was easy for him, even making casual conversation in Spanish, and she was reminded again how much distance and time was between them now. The Daniel she'd loved like a brother and then crushed on like an idiot was different. His life here was so far from the cozy confines of Holly Heights.

To keep this trip on the right track, she needed to cling to the first Daniel, the one who'd seen countless pimples and the horrifyingly bad perm she'd had at sixteen. She would explain to everyone that he was a good friend, nothing more, and then she'd find a new and exotic man in romantic Paris.

Convincing herself that he was only a good friend might make all the difference back in Holly Heights, too. Maybe she'd take the men who sat across from her on dinner dates more seriously.

In a flash they were rung up, checked out and back in the car. "You know, for a guy who's trying to raise money, you haven't pushed your luck. Shouldn't I be bankrolling my own junk food habit?"

She opened the bag of chips and offered it to him.

He took a handful of chips out, started the truck and said, "Don't worry. I'm putting it all on your tab."

The truck lurched as Daniel made the turn on to the dusty gravel road, and she gripped the handle above the door again. He laughed and glanced her way, so she pasted on a confident expression. "Oh, I'm not worried. Thanks to the Big Star lotto, I can cover the tab." A hard jounce shook her across the seat, and she grabbed the bag of chips before it could sail on to the floorboard. The bumps in the road and the crackle of gravel under the tires were loud so Stephanie shut up and held on.

"This more like what you expected?" Daniel asked as he slowed to pass a woman walking beside a donkey. The woman raised a hand to her straw hat.

"It's still pretty flat. That's not what I pictured." She glanced in the side mirror to see the dust cloud fall between the truck and the woman, dimming the bright colors in her wrap.

Daniel pointed over the steering wheel. "Not for long. We're going up." They drove quickly past a small town that seemed nothing more than deserted strips of small homes made of concrete-block walls and tin roofs, crossed a trickle of water that might be a stream on some days, and started winding their way up the mountain. At the first insane hill, Daniel flipped off the air conditioner and rolled down the windows. "This is when the khaki might come in handy. If the dust gets too much…"

What? Let me know? Too bad for you? She wanted to know how that sentence ended but she was too busy biting her lips to ask.

Stephanie was doing pretty well with the whole "faking being totally okay with this speed" thing until he wedged a knee under the steering wheel to twist off the cap of a bottle of Inca Kola. "Here. Try this."

Instead of shrieking at him to concentrate, she studied the bottle.

Calm, Stephanie. He's watching you, waiting for you to freak out and prove him right. Proving him right this early on will make the rest of the trip impossible.

Glass bottle. Cold yellow liquid. How bad could it be?

"Put both hands on the wheel and I will." She took the bottle and very obviously waited for him to comply. When he did, she put the bottle to her lips and took a tentative sip. "Mmm, that's good."

She handed it back and tried not to think about how sharing a bottle was the kind of thing a happy couple might do.

"Definitely worth taking a chance on the unknown now and then." Daniel nodded, tilted the bottle back. For a split second Stephanie was distracted by how good he looked with those muscles, that cold drink and the satisfied sigh. Then she remembered the speed and the road.

Enough was enough. Nagging would confirm his suspicions that she should have been left in a cushy hotel in Lima. But there would be no fun in saying "I told you so" if they were both dead. "Please slow down.

The medical personnel for the area is in this truck so if we crash…"

"No worries. We'd never survive the drop." Daniel's lips were twitching as she gasped out loud. "Come on. This is fun, right? And beautiful."

Daniel pointed and for the first time Stephanie noticed the amazing stretch of mountains ahead of them. Also, the curving road that seemed to completely disappear. The sheer wall of mountain marked one side of the road that was just wide enough for one car with a complete lack of rail on the other side that might prevent them from taking a long drop. Like, a very long drop. Where was the bottom of that fall?

She expected Daniel to comfort her with dry statistics on how few people died by plunging over the side of the road. Brushing off her concern and the real danger took some getting used to.

A cold drink might be the only thing to save her, so she fished a Coke out of her convenience store bag. The first sweet sip was calming.

"What do we do if we meet another car?"

Stephanie asked and bit back a frightened squeak as gravel spun under the truck's tires.

"Negotiate. Very carefully. You'll see." His certainty didn't reassure her.

That's what she'd been afraid of.

Was he trying to frighten her back to Lima? One glimpse of his face convinced her that this was his normal. In fact, he seemed to be enjoying himself.

If he'd wanted peace and quiet for his drive to Alto, he was totally going to get it. She couldn't have made inane conversation about sports teams and weather if her life depended on it. She was too busy swallowing back pleas to slow down and be careful. Be more careful. Please be more careful.

Then the truck lurched, headed for the wall instead of the drop and Daniel cursed. Before she could gather her breath to scream, before the movie of her life began to flash in front of her eyes, he had the truck stopped. "Flat tire." Instead of shouting it like it might be the thing that spelled the end, his voice was flat with annoyance.

As though a flat tire while clinging to the side of a mountain was the same as a hangnail.

Here it might be.

Stephanie glanced wildly over both shoulders as if something might have changed in the two seconds she'd had her eyes squeezed shut. "Here?"

Daniel rested his chin against his chest for a second and then handed her his bottle. "They hardly ever happen on nice, level spots, especially around here." He slid out of the truck, and she put both bottles in the cup holders before she inched her way out between the truck and the dusty mountain.

"But you know how to fix it?" Her fingers ached and she realized she'd tangled them together in a tight ball. At this second, in this place, she was as equipped to change that tire as she was to fly back to Lima. Eventually she might figure it out, but not before they were flattened into more Peruvian dust.

Daniel wrapped both hands around hers, the ones she didn't know she was wringing like a true damsel in distress, until some of his calm and warmth seeped through her skin. He'd always been able to do that, break through her worry and give her some peace.

"Relax. This is business as usual. I can

change it. Haven't I always kept you safe? You and the other Holy Horrors have trained me well. Big brother to the rescue again." He tilted his head to catch her stare, and they stood there for a long minute. "We'll get the tire fixed in the next town. Everything is fine." She matched every deep breath he took and realized that, although he was a brilliant doctor, this ability he had to convince her that everything was going to be okay made him the best.

Then she understood what he'd said. Big brother. Except he wasn't and the way he saw their relationship hadn't changed at all.

But she had.

Or she could if she wanted to, and this trip was her shot to show him and prove it to herself.

Starting right here, on the side of this mountain, where they both might be pulverized together if they didn't get a move on.

"Okay. What can I do to help?" Now that she was breathing properly, she was ready to do whatever she could to get them moving again.

"Get back in the truck." He turned away,

pretty much assuming his order would be carried out quickly.

"Can't get back in the truck. I'm helping." Forcing her hands to her side was a strong first step. From there she could…do something.

When Daniel turned around, his impatience was impossible to miss. He raised a single eyebrow in response.

"I'm lending moral support." She motioned at the narrow space between the truck and the mountainside. "You won't even notice I'm here."

Unexpectedly, his lips were twitching when he let out the long beleaguered sigh that had often been his response to their shenanigans.

"Stay there, between the truck and the mountain. If someone comes around that curve, I don't want you out in the road." He pulled the spare out of the back of the truck along with the jack, and once again she was reminded that now he was the sort of doctor who did heavy lifting. Obviously. Watching him work was pleasant.

"Well, since you asked so nicely…"

Then she focused on what he'd said. Someone else might be coming around that curve? She leaned over the hood to try to gauge the chances of another car making it around them. "We're all going to die."

His rough chuckle was easy to hear even as he worked the jack. "Nobody's going to die. I have patients to see tomorrow."

She thought about explaining how that made absolutely no sense, but she didn't want to distract him. Instead she stared out over the vast space between the road they were on and the amazing mountain opposite them. Nothing but air and dirt and a tiny little ledge that cars and people were supposed to move along.

"Are you still with me?" Daniel asked. He must have had to repeat himself because he was standing next to her, wiping his hands on a towel that couldn't have been much cleaner than his grease-covered palms.

"Ready to go?" The shrill tone didn't please her, but maybe Daniel gave points for effort because he didn't tease her or show any impatience. He nodded, walked around the truck and slid onto the driver's seat.

The cold bottles were sweatier than her hands, but Stephanie took them out of the cup holders and handed him one. "Nice job, Doc."

"I couldn't have done it without your support." His warm smile reminded her of other sunny days, other adventures. Everyone else thought he was so serious.

Was she the only lucky one to see this side?

They clinked the necks and Daniel started the truck. The shot of cold and sweet settled her jitters, and she was able to concentrate on how smoothly he negotiated the road.

"That didn't even bother you, did it? Change a lot of flat tires on your Mercedes back home?"

He yanked off his cap. The wind blew through the window, ruffling his sweaty curls and Stephanie tried to remember if she'd ever seen them before. Daniel wasn't answering her question about his former pride and joy, and she needed a distraction from her calculations on how long they could travel without meeting a car coming the other direction, so she said, "Not breaking any rules. That has nothing to do with Holly Heights Hospital or being fired, although if you'd like to talk about it, we certainly can. If you'd told me what a rotten day you were having, I would have never added to it by propositioning you."

And she might not have to wonder if her invitation, which had bordered on a declaration, was one of the things keeping him away from Holly Heights. The poor guy might have made it home sooner if he hadn't been afraid there'd be a lovesick fan waiting right behind his sister.

"Propositioning me? You asked me to dinner. Choose your words more carefully, English teacher." He navigated a sharp turn in the shadow of the mountain. She watched his lips tighten and he rolled his shoulders slowly. "Flat tires are just another day around here. The first one rattled me, but I've learned I can handle them. That's one good thing about this life. You find out pretty quickly you're capable of more than you ever imagined."

So he was going to skip over the parts he

didn't want to talk about. That made a lot of sense.

She'd already started doing more than she'd imagined. She'd had her doubts whether their friendship would be enough to get her into the truck. If she'd known about the condition of the road, Stephanie was certain she would have believed herself incapable of riding shotgun without gasping at each turn. By the time she landed in Texas again, what else would she be have mastered? "You going to teach me how to change a flat?"

He slowly shook his head. "Not until I show you how to drive on these roads, and neither one of us is up to that." He shot a look at her death grip on the handle over the door. He was right, but she wouldn't let him know that.

"Pretty sure I could handle it." Just like that, she had to eat her words when they met not a car but a truck filled with people coming the other direction. Daniel immediately stopped his truck and eased it back to a dip in the mountain wall. "First rule of passing: hug the mountain."

"Let them take the outside? Got it." They both watched as the truck eased around them with shouts and waves from the passengers, and then Daniel pulled out of the dip and hit the gas.

Stephanie picked up the bag of chips, forced herself to let go of the handle and calmly shoved a handful in her mouth. By the power of carbs, she'd make it through this. When they rolled to a stop in the small main square of the next town, she'd managed to work her way through the bag, her Inca Kola and the Coke. And she felt better.

"Proposition, to propose something, like a date. I am good with words, Dr. Lincoln. In fact, I'd say we've already had our dinner date. We just shared a bag of chips and a drink. That's almost a meal—a really cheap date with spectacular scenery." She waved a careless hand to demonstrate how un-terrified and well-adjusted she was at this point in the trip and her life.

The fact that she'd actively plotted a way to prove her lack of injury, years after the incident, might not support her claims.

"Stay here. Don't move. I'll take you to

the hospital for the restroom as soon as I get the tire patched." Before she could salute smartly, Daniel was out of the truck. She glanced back in time to watch him lift the tire out of the back. He was tall and strong and didn't seem much like the hotshot doctor she remembered. Dirty jeans and tan skin were a good look for him. The dark frown on his face was a lot more familiar. After he walked down the middle of the street and turned the corner, she checked on her suitcase, gasped in dismay over the solid coating of dust, and settled back in her seat.

"Stay here. Don't move," she grumbled. His voice wasn't easy to copy but the frown was. "Big brother or dictator? It's a fine line."

That was when she noticed a line of schoolgirls forming on the sidewalk behind the truck. Dressed in adorable navy and gray uniforms, they watched the truck closely and giggled.

Small town Texas or mountain village in Peru, giggling eight-year-olds must have been universal.

Digging around in her bag from the convenience store, she grabbed the candy she'd picked up and then took her camera out of her backpack. One more glance showed impatient mothers joining the kids. Even better. She could ask permission to give candy and take photos.

If she could remember that much Spanish.

Maybe they knew English.

Stay here. Don't move. Those had been his orders and she couldn't claim she'd forgotten his second rule with a straight face. So this was going to make him mad.

Would he be shocked to learn that his disapproval wouldn't keep her from doing what she wanted? Maybe. She was sort of surprised herself. Living in Holly Heights meant spending a lot of time pleasing the people in her life.

They loved her and wanted the best for her, but the "best" was always safe, predictable and matched what they wanted, too.

The freedom felt so good.

The straggling line of kids dressed in school uniforms was right outside her window, practically begging to be her first adventure in bad Spanish.

She grabbed the candy and eased out of the truck, not quite convinced her plan was solid but more certain staring out the window because she was afraid to take a chance was a serious fail.

No one on the sidewalk moved.

"Would it be okay if I—" She held up the camera and mimed taking shots. The women in charge of the group turned and spoke in rapid-fire Spanish. Stephanie had no hope of keeping up and cursed this trip and its lack of planning. If only she'd had time to cram. Visiting Peru would have been a lot less intimidating if she could do more than ask where the bathroom and library were.

Finally the women agreed and gathered the children into a neat group. The backdrop of the dusty street and the church across the square filled the frame with a real slice of daily life. Stephanie snapped the photo and then turned the camera around to show the women. "Very pretty. *Bonita*."

They nodded and answered her. Waving her hands, Stephanie said, *"Lo siento. No hablo espanol. Malo."* She *was* sorry. The questions she wanted to ask burned on her tongue. This once-in-a-lifetime chance to make friends and her inability to do it would bother her for a long time. More than anything she wanted to ask about school, what they were studying and how they liked it. She could ask the mothers about their days and what it was like living with all this beautiful sunshine.

Meeting people and being unable to connect was torture. She didn't want to let the opportunity slip away.

You won the lottery. There's no reason this has to be your last chance, Stephanie.

Reassured that her dismal language ability wouldn't hold her back forever, she grabbed a handful of candy and offered it to the women. In a heartbeat, the kids had cleared all the inventory and lined up for seconds. Their beautiful grins made it impossible to say no.

While she was rummaging in the truck, the commotion behind her turned from quiet giggles to happy squeals and cries of "Doctor! Doctor!"

She was busted.

Not that she'd had any intention of trying to pretend she'd followed his orders.

Still, it might have been nice to have the choice.

Determined to show him that she was different, even if she had to learn how to be different on this trip, Stephanie straightened her shoulders and tossed a bag of candy to him. "Found it." Then she smiled brightly in response to his complete lack of expression and picked up her shield, the camera.

With the lens between them and a circle of kids surrounding him, his features softened. Instead of impatient, Daniel was happy. Kind. Following the excited conversation was beyond her, but it was clear that he knew these kids, remembered their names and could tease them into more laughter.

She'd seen him striding down the halls of Holly Heights Hospital. In a white coat and a dark tie, he'd been intimidating, even awe-inspiring. The kind of man it was impossible to argue with or doubt.

In his dirty jeans, ragged shirt and messy curls, Daniel looked more like an adventure guide than a man who'd performed complicated surgery in sterile operating rooms.

He also smiled like a man who enjoyed every single minute of his life.

Maybe she wasn't the only one who'd come to Peru to make a change.

She should take a page from his book.

With her luck it would be written in Spanish, but that didn't make reading it impossible.

All she needed was a translator.

CHAPTER FOUR

DANIEL KNEW HE should have expected Stephanie to ignore his rules.

She'd never been afraid to bend the rules to get what she wanted. Most of the time, all she'd needed was a charming grin and an easy laugh. Stephanie was always the spokesperson for the group, and whenever he'd needed to be taken down a notch or two, she was the best at administering the blow almost painlessly. If his sister was a feather, Jen was a hammer and Stephanie was somewhere in between.

Now Stephanie was standing in the middle of a dirt road in the Andes Mountains. She couldn't speak the language, had no concept of the dangers the town or its people might present, and she'd still waded in against his advice.

But she fit perfectly surrounded by happy kids.

Before he'd left Texas, he used to attend

the Friday night football games. After all, the Holly Heights Mustangs were always a strong team. When he'd finished medical school and returned to Holly Heights, he'd been pretty sure watching the hometown heroes tear up the football field was less important than making his mark as a surgeon.

Unless his sister asked.

And he'd been proud to see the way the students flocked around Rebecca, dedicated school counselor, and Stephanie and Jen. Here, Stephanie had managed to spark giggles with a little effort and a jerky conversation made up of a mix of English, Spanish and odd sign language.

He caught her eye and shook his head, reminding her of his second rule, and then focused on his patients. He checked to see how wounds were healing. Bright eyes and clear noses indicated the meds he'd left were working. And all the mothers nodded when he asked about the basics: washing hands, brushing teeth and plenty of time to play. The mothers understood. Following up might help the kids believe, too.

This town, Manzana, was an example of

what clinics could do. It had been his first stop and his focus for the first six months. It was time to schedule a dentist and an optometrist. The beginning of the dry season was the easiest time.

"Stephanie, do me a favor. Make a note. I need to talk to Dr. Wright about a clinic here. Manzana. Before September." Then he gave a little boy, Hector, a high-five. He could hear her thinking loudly in his direction, but to his surprise, she pulled out her journal, made a note and shoved it in her backpack without a single comment.

Growing up, he'd been able to count on hearing exactly what all three girls had thought about his clothes, his hair and his orders whenever it occurred to them.

This time she smiled brightly. "At least you said *favor.*"

"September. It's when the rainy season starts. Hard to travel." He wasn't sure why he was explaining, but she pursed her lips and nodded as if everything made perfect sense. That felt better than it should. "I need to check in at the hospital." He turned to survey the crowd of kids and the people lurking in the small doorways. His arrival always stirred up an audience. Almost never did he have to worry about what to do about it.

This time he had the feeling if he left Stephanie here on her own, she'd either be elected mayor or wind up an accidental bride. "You better come with me. There's a restroom."

Her reluctance to leave the center of town and the excited kids was easy to read. When she walked, she did so slowly. He shook his head, took her hand in his and headed for the hospital.

The gaggle of girls whispering and pointing was his first clue something was up. His second was Stephanie's cheeks, which had turned pink. Her glance at the crowd and then down at their joined hands helped him finally do the math. Amused at how little it took to make them the center of gossip, he squeezed her fingers. "Keep up, okay?"

She wrinkled her nose. "Just like that, a whole town's romantic hopes are dashed on the rocks of impatience."

He shook his head. "Doubt it. They don't speak a lot of English."

Her laugh matched her steps: slow, reluctant, but he was glad to hear it. He squeezed her hand. When she squeezed back, he was surprised at how nice it felt to be holding her hand, his little sister's partner in crime and one of the few women in the world whose good opinion mattered.

Adjusting to the fact that she was standing here on the middle of a dusty street in Peru would take some time.

Since he'd been in Peru, he'd gotten more comfortable as the odd man out. Everyone else was connected in family groups. Other medical crews came and went, but he stayed behind. Being able to do so took some confidence and a lot of discipline, but walking down the street with Stephanie was different.

Stephanie had always grounded him by reminding him someone in the world could see his flaws and like him anyway. Until she'd asked him out on a date, she'd been his second sister.

This Stephanie, the one ready for adventure, whose hand fit his perfectly, was no sister.

But thoughts like that would lead to trouble. Stephanie was here for two weeks. He'd keep her safe, like he would Rebecca if she were riding shotgun, and send her right back home.

"*Hola*, doctor," Gaby Flores said. "I am happy to see you."

She studied Stephanie and their joined hands before she added, "We have a few patients, but I would appreciate your opinion." After she placed the broom she'd been holding in the corner of the dark room, she motioned them to follow her.

"Steph, I'd like you to meet Gaby. She's a nurse, and she runs this clinic. Gaby, this is my friend Stephanie. She's going to walk around, take some pictures." He pointed to the back. "Restroom's back there if you need it."

"I won't take any shots of the patients— just some photos to give your donors an accurate picture of how you work." Her fingers wiggled against his and he realized he was still holding her hand. Now he was the reluctant one. While he had her hand in his, he was fairly sure he could keep her out of trouble.

"Okay. Don't touch anything." When she let go, he made a fist of the hand that suddenly felt awkward.

"I'll only play with the sharp, pointy things. Needles. Scalpels. Things like that. Nothing that can really hurt me, okay, Dad?" She shook her head and walked away muttering.

He watched her for a second and wondered what she'd think of the place. Manzana had one of the best clinics in the area. Right now there were no lights. Generators would run critical machines if needed, but the electricity would come and go during the day. Gaby and the local volunteers made sure the wide open room with beds for patients was kept spotless. At the front were two tiny desks for Gaby and the attendants who helped her overnight, and the small closet at the back held all the medical supplies.

"Gaby, have you made a list of things you need?" He turned on the water, waited for it to turn scalding hot and washed his hands.

"I believe we have what we need, Doctor, but please review the stores before you go."

Gaby brought him three pieces of paper. He scanned them quickly.

"Did you have any trouble with the delivery?" If he recalled correctly, Rosa Vilca had three children already. He hadn't expected her to visit the clinic for the delivery of the fourth.

"A bit." Gaby handed him a stethoscope. "Her blood pressure was very high, but now she seems recovered." She pointed at the readings she'd jotted down.

Gaby was right. He ran a finger down the list to see how the numbers had changed. They moved on to the next patient, and two hours later Daniel was patting the hand of Juan Ramirez, an older gentleman who'd spent too much time in one of these beds.

"I agree with Gaby. As long as that cough continues to improve, you should be home by the weekend." He did his best to gracefully accept the old guy's thanks.

This was not the kind of medicine he'd planned on practicing. Surgeons didn't have to do much bedside comforting. Precision had been all that mattered, not personality. That meant freedom to speak first and carefully consider his words never in Holly Heights.

Not that his bedside manner had been all that bad, but he'd have done better to spend less time talking and more time listening.

Tests and prescriptions and surgeries were rarer now. Here what he said mattered almost more than what he did.

That had taken some getting used to. It was a lot harder to be right when it came to choosing words. Rolling his shoulders to ease some of the tension that built every time he talked with people who needed so much and got by with so little, he walked into the closet that Gaby ruthlessly organized. She must work around the clock.

It was a relief to see fully stocked shelves. That meant there'd be more for the smaller clinic he was still building. "Looks good, Gaby." He realized he hadn't seen or heard Stephanie since she'd muttered away from him. "I have requested nursing staff, and I'm hoping to have résumés to review on my return trip."

"The apartment is ready, Doctor." She smiled. "And I would like to have the help."

Of course she would. She was effectively on-call here in Manzana twenty-four hours a day.

Even in his hotshot days and during his residency, he'd had a chance to stop being a doctor for an hour here and there. Gaby needed support. He would get it for her.

"Thank you for everything you do." Gaby raised an eyebrow and smiled. If his trusty unwanted assistant had been around, he'd have asked her to make another note: thank the people who did the hard work more often.

"Have you seen Stephanie?" Tracking her down wouldn't take long, but he was sort of hoping she hadn't been unsupervised while he'd been lost in his own world.

"I believe she's outside." They stepped on to the sidewalk to see Stephanie managing a small army of helpers. Three girls were gathered around her to put trash in the empty bag she held. Another boy was sweeping the sidewalk in front of the clinic. And their mothers stood off to the side, bemused smiles on their faces.

He understood exactly how they felt.

"How helpful you all are," Gaby said and clapped as the kids surrounded her, their high-pitched voices raised in excitement.

"I told them you would have some treats if they'd like to stop by and help now and then," Stephanie said and shrugged. "I hope that's okay." She picked up her backpack and pulled out the bag of candy she'd shoved inside. "You keep this. I'll buy more bags when we make it to Lima and send them back with Daniel."

Gaby pressed one hand to her cheek as she took the bag. "I will have more help than I know what to do with, but what a happy problem."

Daniel frowned. It couldn't be that simple, could it? In less than an afternoon, Stephanie had figured out a way to get Gaby help. Sure, it was kids. They might be as much work as they were reward, but their parents could be a huge help if they got involved.

Was it true that where kids went, their parents would follow? It was worth finding out.

"Great idea, Steph." He laughed at the shock on her face. Whatever she'd expected, probably frowns and a few grunted orders, he'd surprised her. That was a good feeling.

Except it reminded him of Gaby's surprise.

Was he becoming too predictable? Worse, was he becoming a joyless grump with no time for anything but work? How long would work be enough if that was the case?

He'd joined HealthyAmericas because he wanted to make amends and show the world he wasn't what people said he was. He'd become a doctor for the right reasons, and he'd never forgotten them. He loved what he was doing now.

Except for the fund-raising piece. He'd never been good at making chitchat.

"Uh, thanks, D. I'm filled with good ideas." Stephanie smiled at Gaby and they hugged goodbye. As easy as that Stephanie had made a new friend. Then Gaby stood back and gave him a nice, restrained wave. After a little more than two years, he got a wave. Then, when the kids surrounded Stephanie for a group cuddle, the irritation sparked again.

"We need to go. As it is, we'll be traveling in the dark." She wouldn't like that. He wasn't a big fan of it himself, but it had to be done often enough that he'd learned to handle it.

Stephanie resisted his forceful glare until she'd hugged every last child and mother. Then she hugged Gaby again, handed her the broom, and raced to catch up with him.

"What exactly is your problem?" She panted and managed to bump his shoulder before she fell behind and had to run to catch up again. "I did what you told…me." She gasped. "This time."

He stopped in his tracks to wait for her. She rested both hands on her knees and took a few deep breaths. "And you didn't even say *please* or *favor* like good manners suggest." She took a few slow steps. "What is the deal? I'm not this out of shape. Why can't I breathe?"

"Altitude. We aren't very high yet, but it's a lot higher than you're used to. Take it easy for a minute." Which would be a lot simpler if she wasn't trying to keep up with an irritated jerk. "Sorry. I forgot it would take you a while to get used to the air." He could barely remember the early days when standing up had caused his heart to race, but he should have warned her.

"And you were not a happy camper." This time she took his hand in hers and turned toward the truck. "Want to share or are you going to keep on with the silent disapproval, Dr. Lincoln?"

"You're going to start up the giggling rumor mill again," he said as he swung their hands between them.

She rolled her eyes. "Okay, we'll pretend you aren't avoiding the question then."

"How do you do it? Make friends in literally every corner of the world? You can't even talk to them." And he'd had to work long and hard to gain their confidence. His first few months on the mountain had been discouraging because so many people needed help, his resources had been limited, and instead of hugging him goodbye, people had peeked out at him from doorways and shutters.

Until he'd brought Gaby in. She'd saved the clinic in Manzana. She'd also saved his career.

HealthyAmericas had felt like a last resort, but now he couldn't imagine going back to the way things had been. Ignoring hospital protocols to help a patient in need had probably saved a man's life. At the same time, it had painted a big black X on his résumé. A surgeon with a record of flouting rules and regulations would be a dangerous proposition for any hospital administrator.

But in places such as the Andes, where doctors were needed, he'd had a second chance. And Dr. Wright, who'd started HealthyAmericas as a way to help her mother's family and the people of Peru, had been happy to have his help.

Learning to communicate with his patients, not so much because of the language barrier but because of his own arrogance, had taken some time.

It was too bad he hadn't taken a class to learn Stephanie Yates's proven techniques. Make-a-Friend 101.

Every doctor should be required to take it.

"So you're jealous? Of me?" She sighed. "Now I've heard it all." She was quiet for a minute and he wondered if she was struggling to breathe again. When they made it back to the truck, the setting sun cast a rosy glow over the small park in the center of town. The glass in the town's church sparkled and what had been dusty and dry in the afternoon sun seemed warm and alive. "So beautiful."

The sunshine lit her hair and her small smile, and Daniel couldn't help but agree. She was still dressed like the safari tourist, but he had no doubt she could see the beauty of this place. Did she know how lovely she looked at this moment?

Then Stephanie groaned at the sight of her dusty suitcase.

He chuckled. And things were normal again. She slipped her hand from his, ran a finger through the dust and said, "Thanks for the warning."

After they were both inside the truck and bumping down the road out of town, she said, "It's really easy." He glanced her way. "My secret to making friends. Just care. Ask questions and care about the answers. So few people do, you know. When you meet someone who does that, you want to hold on to them."

Then she looked back out the windshield in time to gasp. "Wow! That road is narrow."

"Did you forget?" He held out a hand. "Can I have one of your Cokes?"

Her frown reminded him of times they'd teased each other over the dinner table. More than once, the competition for the last of his mother's rolls had gotten intense. "I shared my Inca Kola with you, remember?"

"Fine. I guess you're right." She took out the bottle and opened it for him. "Enjoy. I hear we've left the land of Coke behind."

"Not exactly." He might have exaggerated the lack of amenities. He'd have to make sure to accompany her the first time she visited Alto's small store.

Instead of demanding answers, she shook her head, grabbed the last bottle, took a drink and turned away from the passenger window. That was a good idea. The darker it got, the scarier it got. But she'd stuck it out so far. She'd handle the dark, too.

"Did you get any good shots?" He was curious about her impression of the mountains and the clinic in Manzana. Seeing his work through fresh eyes might give him a boost, and some days that could come in handy.

"I think so. It was kind of hard to tell because it was so dark. What's the deal with the electricity?" Everyone who joined him in Alto had the same question. Whether they expected service like they had at home or none at all, the hit-and-miss quality of the electricity here was hard to understand.

"Comes and goes. Just like the water." He didn't dare take his eyes off the road, but he could picture her face at the thought of no running water. He'd been dismayed himself. A flushing toilet was pretty much his line in the sand. Luckily, that had been easy enough to work around.

But she didn't ask.

"Bet the clinic wasn't what you were expecting." Of course it wasn't. She'd probably imagined antiseptic air freshener, cold gray walls, whirring machines interrupted by dings, buzzes and occasional codes, and sterile expressions—that's what he'd been picturing on his first trip. In the US, one hospital might differ from the next in terms of décor, but some things were universal. Manzana wasn't like that.

"I'm not sure I thought about it enough to form an expectation." She pulled her camera out of her backpack. "That's why I'm so happy to have a chance to help with your report. People need to think about these things, you know?"

She was smiling down at the camera as she advanced through her shots. "And you have a real treasure in Gaby. She's the kind of doctor I'd want to find standing next to my bed."

"She's a nurse. But you're absolutely right. She keeps the place going." And she needed help. He had to get it for her.

"Nurse, doctor, she's great. Do you plan to hire local medical staff?" She picked up her journal and jotted down a few notes.

"Well, that's the problem, isn't it? If there was local medical staff, we wouldn't be needed." Peru's health ministry had a shortage of doctors, and few men and women who completed medical school wanted to face the challenges of rural medicine. Now that he knew better what those challenges were, he could appreciate the reluctance.

She was quiet for so long that he wondered if the falling shadows had gotten to her. Once the sun fell behind the mountain range, night crashed down suddenly. And the dark was absolute.

If she was scared now, she'd have a real problem when the sun went down.

"Maybe that's something you should work on. Serving communities is critical, but for the future you should be identifying and training doctors to come back. I'm sure the bigger cities are more attractive, especially to young people, but family might be enough to hold them when money doesn't work."

Before he lurched up the smaller road toward Alto, Daniel stopped the truck. "Write that down. That's something we need to consider." After he'd completed medical school, he'd accepted the offer to return to Holly Heights without hesitation. He'd had other offers from hospitals in bigger cities, places that would have put him closer to his dreams of wealth and the high life. But she was right. Being able to practice close to home and family would be enough to attract the right doctor.

Stephanie tipped down her chin and studied his face. It was almost patient, this expression. But not quite.

He knew what she was waiting for. And she looked very much like a teacher working through an important lesson at that moment. "*Please.* Could you do me a *favor* and write that down?" Daniel said. "You have an excellent theory that I would like to explore when I'm not clinging to the side of the mountain." He tightened his hands on the steering wheel. "In the dark."

She patted his leg and then cleared her throat. "Of course. I know that was difficult for you, but asking for help will get easier. You'll see."

He raised an eyebrow and eased back against the seat. "Thanks."

"You're welcome. I knew I could help." Her smug tone was cute, but he wouldn't tell her that.

He waited for her to notice how little of the road was visible. When she put aside her journal and camera and stretched her legs, he started a countdown.

She didn't disappoint.

"Um, what happened to the road?" The small quiver in her voice betrayed nerves. He hadn't heard anything like it all day, and it had been a long trip filled with unexpected adventures. This fear made perfect sense.

"We only have to drive on the part we can see. No problem." He flicked the headlights up to high beams and back down to show her he could, then he put the truck in gear and slowly navigated the twisting curves that moved up and up and up the mountain. He hated doing this at night, but letting her know that would have been a big mistake. She trusted him.

"Gaby's from Lima. She took a one-year assignment, so I'll either have to find a replacement for her or a way to make her stay. She needs help. Your suggestion has some real promise. If there's one thing I know about medical students, it's that they always need money. Maybe it's a scholarship in exchange for service program." He eased around a corner and waited for her to pick up the conversation.

She took a shaky breath. "Or you could identify kids in the villages you serve who've got an aptitude, sponsor them in exchange for service and hope they make their homes close to family. A one-year contract is good. How much better would it be to find someone who already loves the community?"

"Somebody who loves their village like you love Holly Heights, you mean?" She was a good teacher and she was so solidly woven into the fabric of the town that she'd never leave. History and family and friends and the simple comfort of being home would be hard to break away from. He appreciated that better than he ever thought he would.

Not that she had any reason to leave. Her life suited her perfectly.

When she didn't immediately agree, he wondered if she was still breathing. "You okay?"

"Sure."

Her one-word answer discouraged more questions and, for once, he was willing to let someone else drive the conversation.

He'd drive the truck.

CHAPTER FIVE

IF SHE'D EVER thought riding along this winding road would be easier if she could see less of it, she'd been very, very wrong. The truck's headlights seemed too weak to trust. On one side, the sheer face of the mountain hemmed them in. But on the other side? Absolutely nothing marked the edge except for a long drop.

Screaming at Daniel to stop already would accomplish nothing, so she curled her fingers so tightly into her thighs that she was certain to have bruises and silently enumerated all the ways she was going to kill Jen and Rebecca when she got home. Eventually she'd have to narrow down her list to her top two choices because it was impossible to kill them twice.

"We're doing fine. Take slow, deep breaths." Daniel's face was hard to see in the darkness, but his husky voice reminded her of home and safety and trust. If she could believe anyone's promise, it was his.

"I hope you won't mind when I kill your sister." Her voice sounded shakier than she would have liked, but his laugh settled her panic. She wasn't alone. He was here. And Daniel Lincoln was the kind of guy who did everything expertly.

Except follow orders.

"I do mind, but I understand the urge. Believe me, I understand. If I let her survive sixteen, when all three of you were as unpredictable as Texas rattlesnakes, you can forgive a scary drive in the dark." The truck lurched sharply and he stopped. "Good news, though. We're here."

She held her breath as she twisted in the seat. "How can you tell? This dark looks like all the other dark." She wanted to believe him, but at this point she needed proof.

"That was the washout that fills with rushing water during the rainy season." He leaned over to wrap an arm around her shoulder. In the dark, this close, her heart pounded and it was hard to catch her breath. When she was seventeen, that fluttery, anxious feeling had spelled love. Now she knew better. It was attraction, pure and simple. Not rings and flowers and vows, just the age-old desire to get closer to him. Here he could kiss her. No one would see. And nothing had to change.

He gently turned her to the side. "See that small glow?"

"Electricity?" She didn't mean to sound like someone who'd been lost at sea and just spotted land, but that was exactly how it felt. She was finally sure she was going to live. It had been a big question mark for the past hour.

"Yes. Two places. The faint glow on the edge is the Alto store. If you want to call it that. The other one—" he pointed in the other direction "—is the municipal building, where the mayor works when he works. I guess it's like city hall. There are rooms on the second floor that we rent and we store supplies there. You made it through today."

"You had your doubts, right?" When Daniel's arm slid away, breathing got easier but the weird anxiety that kicked in when things went from friendly to…more pooled in her abdomen. She'd gotten pretty comfortable with the easy camaraderie most of her dates ended with. These jitters were hard to ignore. "That's okay. I did, too. Have my doubts. About surviving. You know, the drive."

"How long were you holding your breath? You sound weird, Steph." His teasing was meant to distract her, comfort her, but she hated the reminder that he knew her well enough to hear her confusion. She needed to do a better job of hiding this crazy attraction, even if she couldn't stop feeling it.

Stephanie cleared her throat. "Not quite long enough. I'm still in this truck. Get us out of here before the lack of oxygen does something worse to my brain."

He put the truck in motion and the headlights showed a long line of buildings along both sides of the narrow road. More dirt road. More buildings. And the rest was darkness until they turned up a steep path. The municipal building sat on a hill above the town.

"The view must be amazing. You know, when you can actually see anything." She would appreciate it better when she could tell where she was stepping. Falling off the side of a mountain had to be worse at night than during the light of day.

The truck lurched to a stop again, and the door to the building opened, spilling bright light across the yard in front. A small group stepped out, broad smiles on their faces.

Stephanie put one hand on her door but hesitated. For most of her life she'd been able to swim freely in a small pond filled with friends and family and people who'd known her parents since before they could walk. Here she had none of that safety.

She wasn't a doctor or a nurse, didn't have any medical training beyond Band-Aid application.

She wasn't even invited. Crashing the party had never been her style, but at this point there was nothing to do but pretend she belonged. Eventually it would be true.

Before she could figure out exactly the right thing to say to get off on the right foot, Daniel yanked open the door. "Scared, Steph? I never would have guessed you had it in you, Miss Congeniality."

"Of course not. I was waiting to see if you

had any manners. I'm glad to see they're there, even if they're usually eclipsed by the orders." She slid out of the truck and smoothed a hand over the vest she was pretty sure identified her as the newbie in town.

"Right. Nice try." Daniel hefted her bag out of the truck bed, wrapped an arm around her waist and guided her across the uneven ground. That connection was enough to steady her nerves so that when he introduced her to the translator, the dentist, the dental hygienist and the nurse who were spending this rotation with him in Alto, she was able to commit the names to memory.

Even if she'd been lucky enough to know every neighbor her whole life, she'd learned a long time ago that people were impressed when she remembered their names after one introduction. Listening carefully had always been one of her secret weapons.

"We've got leftover spaghetti and garlic bread if you're hungry," Teresa said as she led Stephanie inside. "My mother's recipe." She waved her hand. "With a few necessary modifications. If she knew I was using garlic flakes, she'd smack my hand with a wooden spoon."

Stephanie smoothed the hair out of her face, refusing to think about the dusty, windblown fashion she had to be sporting after hours in the truck. If she had to guess, Teresa, who was Daniel's nurse, wouldn't judge her too harshly. Her gray hair was piled on her head in a messy topknot and her canvas apron had a red smear down the side. Rebecca of the crisp ruffled apron would be ashamed of herself for such a mess.

Stephanie thought it might be a good sign she and Teresa had some things in common. "Spaghetti. That doesn't quite fit my mental image. I expected energy bars and military-grade prepackaged food. What can I do to help?"

Teresa sighed. "If it was up to Daniel, that's what you'd get. But something I learned about two days into nursing school was that everything's better with good food, even new places and being away from family. Once he tasted my chocolate cake, he was pretty easy to convince."

"I bet." Stephanie turned in a slow circle to take in the cramped kitchen. "All the comforts of home, though." A large water cooler took up one corner and an ancient refrigerator the other. Wedged in between was the stove with a pot simmering on top. The rickety table in front of the door had exactly five chairs and a stack of plates, silverware and cups. Five of each.

"I should have brought my own place setting."

"All the comforts of home save one: a dishwasher. As long as you don't mind dishpan hands, we've got plenty to go around. And Luis, the translator, has his own place. His wife cooks and she must be pretty good. Since we finished up the week's inventory and reading through the list of requests from the last time we made the rounds, he'll be gone, gone, gone." After filling a plate with spaghetti, Teresa pulled out a chair and urged her to sit. "What's your specialty? I was hoping for someone to help with vision tests this time around. We have some glasses left over that you can comb through, add them to whatever you brought."

Stephanie took a bite and then closed her

eyes. "Oh my. This is good." She took another bite and then remembered Teresa had asked her a question. "Sorry. Um, I'm not a doctor. I have no medical training. I'm an English teacher." She focused on her plate and waited for the next question. Eventually she looked up to see the older woman sitting next to her, waiting patiently, her chin propped on her hand.

"And I'm a friend of Daniel's. I'm here to deliver a donation and help with the fundraising report he's working on." She pointed to the backpack she'd abandoned as soon as she'd smelled garlic. "I've got a camera. A journal. And you guys can find a way to use me, too. I like to help."

Teresa patted her hand. "One thing is for sure around here, there's work to be done. I already have an idea." Before Stephanie could ask for more info, Teresa was out of her chair and out of the room. She had to be talking to Nicole, the hygienist, and Dr. Weaver, the dentist, because every now and then she heard words such as "toothbrush" and "floss" and "kids" and "waiting."

Teaching kids to brush and floss might

not have been on her list of things to do, but it would be nice to show Daniel she could do more than stay out of the way.

"It's going to be hard to say goodbye to Teresa." Daniel squeezed around the table and filled his own plate before he sat across from her. "I've never eaten this well here. You picked a good time to visit."

"Sounds like she's making plans for me, too." Stephanie propped her elbows on the table and watched Daniel plow through the pile of noodles on his plate. She was happy he was distracted. The difference in him still caught her off guard. Instead of starched and manicured and arrogantly successful, he was dusty and scruffy, in terrible need of a haircut, and thrilled to sit down with a good plate of food. Forget the expensive car. Never mind the accolades or the respect. Here he had spaghetti and life was good.

Unfortunately, that only made him more attractive.

She might be in real trouble.

Two weeks. Surely protecting her heart for two weeks would be easy enough.

"What? Am I making a mess?" Daniel

wiped his mouth with his hand. "No napkin. I'm hungry."

Stephanie stretched to grab a paper towel. "Nothing. I never expected this food or this place or these people, but nothing is as surprising as the change I see in you."

"Not quite the catch I was, am I?" He shrugged and she was glad he was paying more attention to his plate than to her. She didn't want to ask if he could see how she'd changed, too.

Worse, she didn't want to tell him that this new guy was twice as swoon worthy as the old guy. Just today she'd watched him do heavy lifting and scary driving with extreme competence and comfort young and old alike in a way that would have been impossible for him even to consider before. His orders lacked the air of being stone-tablet worthy that he'd had as an annoying older brother in the early days.

He'd gotten better with time and adversity.

Luckily she'd gotten smarter... Maybe.

Considering the way she was gazing at a man slurping up noodles, probably not. Spaghetti had to be the least romantic food in the world. Not even Daniel could eat it gracefully and still she was admiring his strong arms and the way his curls fell.

Had she killed brain cells by holding her breath? She wasn't that teenager in love with love anymore.

He'd made his feelings clear enough anyway. She was a friend. Never more than a friend.

And Daniel had no interest in kissing his friend.

"This reminds me of Friday nights at Sala Italiana." Daniel stood up to fill a bottle with water from the cooler. "Remember? Everyone else wanted pizza, and you had to rock the boat."

Stephanie shrugged. "The pasta came with bread. I will always choose bread."

"That place has the best sauce. Not better than Teresa's, but definitely the best in east Texas."

"Had." Stephanie watched him carefully. "It closed last year. There was a fire and the owners never rebuilt. Now, for pasta, you have to go to the Bunkhouse." She shook her head. "Believe me, there's nothing authentic and hardly anything Italian about the place."

Instead of eating as if he was afraid someone would snatch away his plate, Daniel moved noodles around on his plate. "So the Sala Italiana is gone. Somehow that bit of news didn't make it this far." He tried a smile. "What else have I missed?"

Stephanie squeezed her eyes shut and tried to come up with something newsworthy. "The old soda fountain is a shiny new service station complete with a McDonald's inside. The Holly Heights bank has changed hands. And the clock over the courthouse has been fixed."

When she opened her eyes again, he'd slumped back against the chair.

"So, you haven't missed much." She sighed. "Well, there are three new millionaires in town. Maybe we ought to open up a new Italian restaurant."

He didn't laugh but nodded when she raised her eyebrows at him. "We'll force this recipe out of Teresa before you leave. That should help." For some reason, he seemed… sad, maybe.

"Everything okay?" The urge to hug him was hard to fight.

She carefully scooted back from the table and ran water in the tiny sink. With as much garlic as she'd consumed, kissing anyone should be the last thing on her mind. Unfortunately, Daniel picked that second to ease up next to her.

"I guess I have a hard time dealing with the fact that Holly Heights is changing without me. I think I'm keeping up with phone calls and emails and Facebook updates, but... I'm not. Not really."

Unable to resist, Stephanie awkwardly patted his shoulder. "Well, sure, but it's not like you wouldn't recognize the place. Holly Heights is still there."

"For how long? If I wait five years, will it still look like home?" He turned off the water that threatened to overflow the sink.

"Maybe it won't be home in five years." Stephanie watched him closely to try to gauge the chances that Rebecca would get what she wanted: her brother's return to Texas. His frown didn't change. "Or maybe home is more about people than a place.

You're keeping up with Rebecca and your parents. You'll always be close to them."

His arm brushed hers as he eased her aside, causing her to jerk in surprise. "I'll wash. You go unpack."

Instead of standing there with her mouth hanging open while she blinked stupidly— or worse, baldly telling him Holly Heights wasn't the only thing that was different— Stephanie turned on one heel and wandered back out into the large open space where the rest of the group sat around a card table.

She did her best to ignore the lingering heat where his hand had rested on her bare skin.

Teresa stood. "Ready to see the rest of the place?"

"Ah, sure," Stephanie said as she walked over to grab the handle of her suitcase. Someone had done his best to wipe off the solid layer of dust. She and Teresa traded turns hauling it up the narrow stairs until they made it to a large room lined with bunk beds.

"Got our own bathroom," Teresa said and opened the narrow door with a flourish. "Comes complete with a shower with two temperatures: fiery hot and freezing cold. But hot water lasts as long as the electricity is on. How long are you planning to stay?"

"Until Daniel heads back to Lima. Two weeks?" Stephanie poked her head in the bathroom to see a toilet, a sink and a shower. She'd be able to wash her hair in the shower and brush her teeth in the sink all while sitting on the toilet. "Handy."

Teresa laughed. "Here's the switch if you ever want to go for boil." She pointed at a button on a contraption over the showerhead.

Stephanie wondered which daredevil inventor figured out how to use electricity in the shower.

"What's the barrel for?" A large blue barrel took up precious space in the corner of the shower.

"It collects water for when the water stops running." Teresa shrugged. "During the dry season especially, the water comes and goes. Flushing the toilet is a must, am I right? Use a bucket, the water in this barrel and gravity when all else fails." Teresa patted her on the shoulder and eased past her. "You can do anything for two weeks."

Stephanie took a deep breath. Teresa was absolutely right, and they'd already done the hard part and worked out a system that made it easier to live here. This would be a challenge but not impossible. "Did I appear terrified? I might be doing that a lot for the next few days."

"Just because it's different, doesn't mean it's bad. You seem like somebody who can get that pretty quickly. I'm not worried so you shouldn't be, either." Teresa pointed at the lone twin bed along the wall. "You might want to claim that one. I don't know that there are any more travelers coming through."

Stephanie eased down on the mattress, not quite sure where to start.

"We'll be playing cards if you want to come down. Daniel never plays, but the rest of us have gotten pretty cutthroat at gin. Got any card skills?" Teresa propped a shoulder against the doorframe.

"Some." She wasn't quite as good at cards as she was at darts, but she, Rebecca, and Jen had forced Daniel to join them at the card table more than once. For a second she wondered why he didn't play here.

Too busy maybe.

"But I was never as good as Daniel." He'd been good at everything, even the card games he didn't want to play.

"Well, if we can ever get him to slow down, we might find out. I guarantee you, as soon as he unloads the truck, he'll be ready to make the plan for the week." Teresa shook her head. "It doesn't change much, but preparation is something he never eases up on. There's a checklist for everything. I guess that's why he's good."

Thinking he'd have more time to play cards if he had help with some of that preparation, Stephanie opened her suitcase to make sure nothing needed her attention. "You know, I could go see what I can do to help. The guy's a cardsharp. I bet I can get him to put on a display of his skills." Sometimes volunteering for the hard jobs caused other people to jump on board, too. Other times, she'd been left doing the work all by herself.

But this wasn't the Christmas parade.

There was no shovel or horse in sight. And Daniel's work was important.

Teresa pursed her lips. "Hmm, we're about to see a new side of the good doctor. He's not an easy guy to help." She smiled. "Anything going on between you two?"

"His sister's my best friend. We've known each other since before I could drive." Stephanie shoved her hands in her pockets, unwilling to give the impression that she'd ever wanted anything else. "We might as well be related."

But the words "big brother" would not pass her lips.

Daniel would probably say it himself soon enough.

Teresa frowned. "That's not the vibe I got when he introduced you. My brother would have insulted me a dozen times in less than five minutes, all the while beaming with pride. Maybe that's just us. Daniel seemed a little…nervous. Like it matters to him how you fit here." She shrugged. "It was kind of sweet. Unexpected, but sweet."

Stephanie wasn't sure how to answer so she was relieved when Teresa waved and turned to go back downstairs. Instead of rushing to follow, she sat down, braced her hands on her knees and studied the dusty linoleum floor. Nothing was working out like she'd expected it to.

She'd successfully talked her way into the trip to Alto. When Rebecca had sprung the idea on her, Stephanie's first thought was that Daniel would hand-deliver her back to the airport with a ticket pinned to her coat. Being bothered by an unexpected responsibility would destroy his plans, and he'd never been good at making adjustments.

But she and Daniel had spent the afternoon together and she hadn't once doodled her first name with his last. Sure, she'd had a weak moment in the kitchen. And before that in the truck. But she'd managed to hold it all together.

She'd thought pretending to be absolutely, perfectly fine with him would be the biggest challenge and had pep-talked herself accordingly on the long flight to Lima.

Discovering it was possible to pretend friendly indifference was nice.

Realizing that the biggest challenge came

from the ways he'd changed was harder to wrap her head around. Like, if he'd been the same old Daniel, the one who'd shot her down so efficiently, she would have felt nothing more than friendship. There were flashes of the old arrogance, but mixing those in with this humbler, more real Daniel made her nervous. Before he'd been a sort of ideal, only in her sights because of their shared history.

Now he was a guy a regular girl like her might fall in love with.

Not admire from afar. Not build daydreams around. But truly learn to admire above and beyond the way he filled out an expensive suit.

Or in this case, dusty denim and old cotton.

She couldn't think of another man who appealed to her the way Daniel did. Was it because he was not an option? Wanting what she couldn't have didn't seem her style, but maybe that was part of her dating problem.

"Two weeks, Yates. You can stay out of trouble for that long. Then, when you sip wine at a street café in Paris, you can pick and choose the men like the perfect bite from a chocolate sampler."

Spunky kid sister. Channel Stephanie Yates, spunky kid sister, for two weeks. She'd satisfy Rebecca and Jen, leave a fat check to make a difference, and celebrate by slaughtering some French words and croissants.

Before she went home, stepped back into her routine and tried to be satisfied with the way things were.

She was still shaking her head as she trotted down the stairs. With the money she'd won she could certainly change her own world. There was no reason to do what she'd always done unless it made her happy.

Maybe that was what these two weeks were really about: figuring out what would make her happy.

Not safe. Not good. Not comfortably meeting every expectation so she could please the people who knew her and loved her. And not Daniel Lincoln.

Figuring out what would make her happy.

That could be a bigger challenge than not falling in love with Daniel.

She wondered if she'd be successful at either.

CHAPTER SIX

DANIEL RAN HIS hands through his hair and stared long and hard at the mirror. "Routine. Stick to the routine." After spending the day with Stephanie and working with her to unload the supplies he'd picked up in Lima, she'd somehow matched his rhythm perfectly. If they were dancing, she'd be an excellent partner. Talking with her was as easy as it ever was, with the exception of that one conversation in his office, but every now and then, the little sister he remembered was replaced with an independent woman whose challenges were more than simply irritating.

Trying to give orders to a smart, logical woman was an exercise in frustration, but in just one day, she'd made him reconsider some things he'd been certain of before he ran into her in Lima.

Instead of staring up at the ceiling all

night and worrying about what he was missing at home, he'd gone to sleep with a smile on his face at the memory of how she'd trounced the whole team after a blistering round of gin and did the required victory dance—the one she, Rebecca and Jen had made up in his parents' living room. He'd always been able to defeat them at darts or cards, but that hadn't stopped them from celebrating second place.

Watching the people who'd been working alongside him for weeks howl with laughter at something Stephanie said almost made this place feel like home. If they'd had no history, all he would see was a beautiful smile that swiftly changed to a wicked grin, and he would be both annoyed and amused at how smart she was.

If things had turned out differently and he was still a hotshot doctor with a view to ruling Holly Heights Hospital, would he have been able to tell this woman no?

This morning he had to get his head on straight. He'd woken up with the thought that he needed to find some time to show Stephanie the hydroelectric plant on the Cañete River. Then he had a minute of clarity. Other than being a huge fan of electricity itself, Stephanie would have no real interest in how it came to be.

Was he searching for tourist attractions? Some way to show off and impress a pretty girl?

As if he was seventeen again.

He needed to get a grip.

He was all about medicine now. Doing the job he'd left home for should be enough.

"Do the job. Make a difference." He'd told himself that countless times. Whenever homesickness made him want to check job openings in the continental US or the fear that he was failing the people he served shook him, he gave himself the same pep talk.

Weaver, the dentist sharing the men's dorm, had gone down to start the coffee. No matter how many people came and went on his rotations, the coffee drinkers were always the minority.

If the decaffeinated understood how beautiful the cool morning could be with a view of the valley below Alto and a hot cup of coffee, he'd have to fight for a cup.

When he made it to the cramped kitchen he was surprised to see Stephanie manning the stove and pouring mugs of coffee. "Don't look so shocked, Daniel." She shrugged at Weaver, Nicole and the translator, Luis, who were crammed around the table. "I can't cook. Never had to, thanks to Daniel's sister, but even I can scramble eggs." She handed him a cup. "Black, right?"

Daniel took it and sipped carefully. Good coffee made beautiful days better.

Bad coffee could derail the whole week.

But this was excellent coffee. Stephanie handed Weaver his cup and then started dishing up plates of eggs while Teresa buttered toast. "If I can swing the breakfast shift, someone else will make sure I don't starve at dinner time."

"I'm glad to have a chance to eat something I didn't cook," Teresa said and grabbed a couple slices of toast.

When he'd first started, he'd ruthlessly divided up all chores. He hadn't wanted to be responsible for cooking any more than he had to, mainly because he didn't want his teams to suffer. Then Teresa had come along, taken one bite of his terrible meat loaf and redistributed the chores immediately.

Teresa did all the cooking. Weaver handled the trash and floors. Nicole did laundry and bathrooms. And he washed dishes.

It suited them all. Teresa's rotation was coming to an end, so he sometimes worried about who would feed the team next.

Then a real crisis would hit so he could gratefully push that concern to the back burner.

"What's on the schedule today? Have pen, will travel." Stephanie leaned against the stove and ate scrambled eggs from the pan.

"Here. Take my chair." Daniel started to ease up to avoid shaking the rickety table but Stephanie waved him back.

"No way. Eat your breakfast." She motioned with a piece of toast. "I've got this under control."

He settled back down, uneasy at the thought of her standing while he sat. It was good to know that thousands of miles from home, he still remembered the lessons his mother had drilled into his head.

"Today we're going to Plata. We've got a

medical clinic planned, and Weaver and Nicole will work through any dental screenings that show up."

When Weaver and Nicole both moaned out loud, he knew exactly why. Some places they went were rough drives, but several villages could be reached only on foot. Plata was one of those places. They'd have to carry in everything they needed.

And they'd be carrying it way, way up.

"Yeah, it's a hard hike, so Stephanie, you stay here. You can make some plans for the report." From safely inside the dorm room. He never worried for his own safety here, but Stephanie might be a novelty the bad guys couldn't resist.

Whoever the bad guys might be.

He was responsible for her safety now, and his sister would murder him if anything happened to Stephanie.

He'd be happy to let her.

But Stephanie wouldn't make it easy on him. He could see the gleam of "Oh, really?" flaring in her eyes.

"No way. That's not the deal. I'm here for the full Peruvian experience. And I can work on the report if I'm with you." Stephanie cocked her head to the side. "It's hard to argue with facts like that."

"Except it's a long, hard hike in and out. We can't drive in, Steph, and you saw the way the others reacted. They know. And they'd get out of it if they could." Weaver and Nicole nodded vigorously while Luis pursed his lips and then agreed. Daniel shook his head. "When we drive to Omas you can get plenty of pictures there."

"Give me a shot to prove you wrong," Stephanie said as she cleared the table. "I jog, you know. I'm totally fit."

He believed she jogged. Now and then. But she was no runner. Still, she was strong and healthy, bright intelligence and enthusiasm lit her face, and her long blond ponytail swung back and forth as she hustled around the kitchen.

Trusting her was easy. Trusting himself to keep her safe was a lot harder.

She smiled as she glanced over her shoulder. "Give it up, Dr. Lincoln. I see the surrender written all over your peevish face."

"Peevish?" Luis repeated the word slowly.

"Annoyed. It's kind of an English major word." Teresa rolled her eyes.

Weaver cleared his throat and Nicole's lips were twitching. They stood. "Ready in fifteen, Daniel," Weaver said and danced a few steps with Stephanie to make his way to the door.

"Are you finished?" Stephanie asked, one hand held out for his plate.

"Sure, but I've got the dishes." Daniel noticed everyone else had already dispersed. He'd been too busy trying to figure out how he'd lost control of the group. "And I am still in charge around here."

"Of course you are. You go do doctor-y things. My backpack is ready." She hummed as she filled the sink and rattled the dishes. Dismissed, Daniel went out to join Teresa, who was packing the medical supplies they'd carry to Plata.

Normally he'd go over every single bag she packed and double-check the supply list he'd crafted for each town they visited. He could tell from the way she clasped her hands and stepped back that she was prepared for him to do the same thing that morning.

But she'd packed the bags every day for almost two months. Was it necessary for him to make sure she'd done it the way he expected? How many times had he made any changes?

"Got it under control, Teresa?" He motioned vaguely at the bags. "Let me know if you need any help."

She blinked in response and then shook her head. "No, we've got everything on the list. I'll go see if Dr. Weaver or Nicole has any additions."

Daniel nodded. "Good." He watched her go and fought the urge to make sure she'd done things correctly.

Stephanie saved him again. "Ready to roll." She clapped her hands. "Where is everyone?"

"Packing supplies. We have to carry in everything we need." He'd give it one last shot. "You know, no one will think any less of you if you stay here, take it easy."

"Which never once occurred to me. I just

thought I could find a way to help." Stephanie winked. "And I will, D. Don't you worry."

Before he could remind her of the rules, particularly the one about following his orders, the rest of the team joined them. They were quiet as everyone grabbed a bag and headed for the truck. With some negotiation, everyone managed to cram inside the cab except Luis, who took one look, shook his head and climbed in the truck bed.

Daniel stopped Stephanie's offer to ride in the back with one solid shake of his head. She challenged him with a glare and then clambered into the middle of the backseat.

"At least I don't have to worry about falling out," Stephanie said cheerfully, her shoulders hovering under her ears in the effort to make more room for Teresa and Nicole. She definitely wasn't going anywhere.

"Everyone's got a water bottle, energy bars, jacket and hat, right?" Daniel asked as he started the truck and waited for the affirmative. "We've got the medical supplies, the dental supplies and enough candy to hand out?"

Again everyone nodded, and he caught

Teresa's glance at Stephanie. Neither of them said anything, but he was pretty sure they were communicating the way women often did when confronted with a man who was being silly. So he shut up, turned the truck around and started the climb to Plata.

STEPHANIE TRIED NOT to bounce into either Teresa or Nicole, but the road got rougher the higher they went. Each lurch and thunk of the truck hitting something made her more nervous, her heart beating heavily in her chest.

The road also got narrower, but she tried not to think about that. They made it through the main street of Alto quickly. Since the road was absolutely deserted, no traffic slowed them down. The only movement she saw came from a pair of chickens standing in a doorway.

"This isn't some zombie ghost town, is it?" She craned her neck to stare out the back window. "Where are the people?"

"My guess is they're working. There are apple trees and crops down by the river." Teresa pointed. "Way down."

"The rest are probably watching us. Carefully." Nicole shrugged and shook all of them in the backseat. "Everybody's got a hobby, you know?"

They wound around and up, the view getting more spectacular with each curve. The mountains in the distance seemed untouched, and even the green valley below showed almost no sign of human interference. "It's like we're the only people on the planet. Ever."

As a suburban girl, Stephanie needed a little time to understand that even in this untouched part of the world, life went on. It was beautiful. And eye-opening.

Eventually, Daniel rolled to a stop.

One glimpse of the road ahead was all it took to understand why.

"Single file, then," Stephanie murmured as she surveyed the ledge that wound along the mountainside and disappeared around a bend. "I'm going to need a spotter, a harness and a tranquilizer."

"What's that?" Daniel asked as he glanced over his shoulder.

"Nothing. I'm all set." She motioned everyone else in the group ahead, crossed her fingers and muttered a fervent wish that she be able to keep up. She'd made some pretty big promises. Keeping them was going to be harder than she'd expected.

She definitely shouldn't have overstated her jogging ability. She did jog, but not if she could help it.

And her heart was already pounding before she took the first step.

Daniel studied her face for a long second. "Weaver, you take the lead."

After the rest of the group headed down the path, unwisely walking closer to the edge than she'd recommend, Stephanie followed and tried to ignore the added pressure of strong, tall, fit Daniel Lincoln walking close behind. The first time she stumbled, he said, "Walk closer to the middle. Hugging the side like that means more rocks."

She wanted to say something breezy and chuckle in an unconcerned manner to make sure he got that she was killing this hike.

But it was hard to breathe.

So she put her head down to watch carefully for any stray boulders and concentrated on taking deep breaths.

Until her heart started racing. And her hands went numb.

When she couldn't feel her feet anymore, things got serious.

"I need…" Stephanie rested against the sheer mountainside and slid down slowly to sit in the dirt. "To stop."

Daniel immediately knelt beside her, one hand on her wrist to take her pulse. "Talk to me."

"Catching my breath." Stephanie considered lying down, studied the rocky, narrow path and closed her eyes instead. The pounding in her head convinced her. She slowly slid down and stretched out along the path, one shoe lace dangling over the edge. There in the shade, it was blessedly cool.

Closing her eyes meant she couldn't see five other people staring down at her with concern.

She'd also miss Daniel's smug "I told you so" and, even if she deserved it, that was a bonus.

If the movie of her life started rolling, she didn't want to miss the early years.

After a few deep breaths in and out, breathing got easier. Her heart, instead of hammering in panic against her chest, thudded heavily and she could hear blood rushing.

Daniel lifted her head out of the dirt to rest on his leg. His warm palm against her clammy forehead was a pleasure.

"You go on. We'll rest here for a few more minutes." Stephanie cracked one eye open to see him waving at the rest of the group. "I can catch up."

Not we. *I can catch up. Way to go, little sister.*

Teresa patted Stephanie's shoulder and said, "Take it easy, okay?" before she turned to follow the rest of the group.

Daniel didn't say anything else but watched them turn the corner of the path and disappear.

"You go, too. I'm fine. I can sit here forever or until you guys come back." Stephanie was pleased to see her hands still worked when she took the water bottle he offered.

Uncertain whether it was a good idea to stop breathing long enough to take a drink, she waved the other hand. "Really. I'm fine. I'll go back to the truck and take a nap or something."

One warm hand braced under her neck made it easier to sit up and take a drink of the sweet, cool water.

Daniel shook his head. "No way. If we can get you to the truck, I'll take you back to Alto."

Stephanie gulped down the water and took inventory. Hands: working. Feet: tingling awake. Heart: still beating. If she could get control of her breathing, she could make a second attempt. She'd sworn she could handle this and if she failed, she was certain to hear about it every time a similar showdown occurred for the rest of forever.

She eased up to sit next to Daniel.

He didn't speak, just tapped the water bottle. She got the message and took another long sip.

"Okay, while I'm recovering, let me have it. I deserve an I-told-you-so of epic proportions." She closed her eyes and leaned her head back against the mountainside. If she were in her right mind, she'd be worried about Andean insect life, dirt in her hair and the threat of another seriously cold shower, but she wasn't.

"Things are different here. The distance is easy but the altitude is no joke." Daniel took a long drink of water. "Next time you'll find this easier."

"That's it? No lecture?"

"You seem to think I'm arrogant. Bossy. A know-it-all. Why would you waste your time asking me to dinner in the first place? I sound like the worst kind of jerk." He didn't look her direction, just crossed his legs slowly and waited.

Jen had asked her the same question when she'd confessed her error in judgment.

"If the worst kind of jerk is intent on sin-gle-handedly saving the world." Stephanie wrinkled her nose at him, hoping he'd relax a little. They were tiptoeing closer to break-ing one of his rules. "Plus, you're handsome. Even if you know it, you're still good-look-ing."

"So I'm like a hot supervillain but without all the cool gadgets?" Daniel pointed at his bag. "Well, a few cool gadgets, I guess."

"More like a hero who needs to learn to delegate. What you need is a faithful sidekick." Stephanie flexed her toes and was pleased to see her muscles were cooperating again. Instead of solid lumps of pain, they were at least pliable.

"A faithful sidekick like you, you mean?" He shook his head.

"I'm no sidekick, sweetie." She patted his leg. "Get me back on flat ground and I'll show you I've got some power of my own. And if you aren't going to tell me how I've messed up your plans for the day or how many children will miss their vaccinations because I insisted on having my way or any of the other things I'm using to beat myself up, we should get moving."

She'd slowed him down, something she'd promised herself and him she wouldn't do. He had an important job. Maybe she could learn to listen to his orders and follow the ones that might actually matter.

"I don't have to say any of those things." Daniel reached up to rub the tense muscles across her shoulders and the headache eased. "I could see the panic and regret on your face. There's no room for I-told-you-so at that point. I learned that the hard way." He shrugged. "Could be it even made me a better person, making a mistake that one time."

They both laughed. A few hundred questions and reassurances and promises hovered at the tip of her tongue. His mentioning the reason he'd left Texas and retreated to these mountains opened the door a crack to talk about his mistake at Holly Heights. "Caring too much might lead to mistakes, Daniel, but it's definitely a fine quality in a doctor."

When Rebecca had first told her he'd been fired, she'd fought the urge to storm into the hospital, ready to do battle on his account. And before she could figure out how to swallow her pride and offer him her support like a normal person, a good friend, he'd been gone.

"At some point, figuring out that I'm not the only one who can save the world will make my life easier. I think." Daniel didn't turn toward her. "If I'd done it sooner I might still have the job, might still be at home."

"Everyone makes mistakes." Stephanie rubbed the ache at her temple. "That doesn't mean you can't have the life you wanted."

Daniel didn't answer for a long moment. "If anyone could convince me of that, it would be you."

His eyes were serious. Refusing to jerk in surprise took every bit of strength she had. She wanted to ask if he meant that in a "you're stubborn enough to get what you want" kind of way or if he meant something more.

Did he sometimes wish he'd said yes to a date with her?

Would she have been able to convert a friend into something more?

Stephanie had the feeling the shifting sand was going to get treacherous. She was already clinging to the side of a mountain, which would make baring her soul a challenge.

Plus, she was a chicken. This Peru adventure was using up every single bit of her bravery reserves. She didn't have it in her to ask him again for something more. Not here. Not now.

If he carefully explained why more between them was such a ridiculous dream, she might jump off the edge. And if he laughed as though she was making a joke again, she might give him a push.

She had no desire to live with that guilt for the rest of her life.

"How far is Plata?" She stared long and hard at the path. It seemed to end in midair.

"Around that corner, and up." Daniel was looking in the other direction, at the truck in the distance. His plan was clear. In his mind she was already heading back down the mountain.

"All right. I think I can do it." Stephanie did not want to do it. But she had to. And she'd done one or two hard things she didn't want to do in the past. When she conquered this one, she'd have a badge of honor.

"No way. The altitude is too much for you. And that's nothing to be embarrassed about, Steph. After some acclimation this will get easier." Daniel pressed his fingers over her pulse again. "Better."

Instead of letting go, he tangled his fingers with hers. "Drink more water. Then we'll get you back to the truck."

To please him, she followed orders. When he stood and offered her both hands to help her up, she said, "I'm going to try this one more time."

The second he started shaking his head, she countered by nodding vigorously. "I know you think you're the big brother, the boss, here, but you aren't my brother." She rubbed her forehead. "Or my boss either, for that matter. You don't have to protect me from myself, Daniel. I know I can do it. This is happening."

At some point, she had to prove to them both that things had changed. This could be a good start.

If she actually survived.

His lips were a tight, disapproving line, but Daniel waved a hand in front of him. "Nothing's easy with you. If you go farther down this path, it'll be harder to get you back to the truck."

Excellent point. Stephanie studied the disappearing track, took another physical inventory, ignored the way her legs felt like stumps after all the adrenaline had disappeared and started walking. Slowly, they made it along the path. She stopped twice to flop in the dirt, but Stephanie was proud of herself for refusing to beg him to leave her there. In the dirt. Clinging to the side of the mountain on a path wide enough that she could rest against the side and see over the edge.

Eventually they turned the corner. The path didn't disappear, but there were steps cut into the mountain. "Oh. Good. Steps."

Daniel shifted back and forth. "Maybe I should have mentioned that. I didn't know it would be the final straw."

"Nope. I can do it, but I won't think about how I have to get back down these at some point." Unless she decided to stay. Forever. Maybe Plata was a beautiful place and she could have all her mail forwarded.

The climb was scary, but after the hike she figured she had nothing to lose, and before she knew it, she was kneeling at the top of the steps and staring at a small, neat village.

"I did it." What she wanted to do was stretch out in the shady spot next to the scratching chickens so she could celebrate every breath. Instead she forced herself to stand up and smile as Daniel climbed the steps to stand next to her. He studied her face carefully for a long second. Then he shook his head, the small smile on his face lighting up his eyes and making him seem younger, more handsome.

If that was even possible.

"So, we know you've got grit." He pulled a long blond hank of hair over her shoulder. "Also, you're covered in dirt from head to toe."

"Dirt washes. This victory will stick with me." She took the backpack that he'd somehow thrown over his own shoulder, on top of his heavy bag of supplies. "Take a picture of me. I don't want to ever forget this. And I want proof to show Rebecca and Jen. They won't take my word for it. I wouldn't believe me myself."

"Really. Didn't sound like you had any doubts when you were making your stand." He waved his hands. "But I'm not your brother or your boss, just the guy who's done this before."

"And I appreciate your concern. It's just not your job to smother me anymore. Take the picture."

His mouth dropped open. "Smother?"

"Okay, coddle. With love. Take the picture." She handed him the camera, flexed her biceps to strike a pose and waited for the snap.

He snorted but his grin broadened as he gave back the camera. "You scared me. I wouldn't have thought any less of you if you'd wanted to go back." He wrapped his arms around her and squeezed her tightly against his chest.

The wish that he'd done this when she wasn't covered in a fine layer of dirt and smelling of fear was quickly chased away by the realization that Daniel Lincoln had his arms around her, that she was pressed close to this man she'd once imagined to be perfection.

Now he had enough scruff to qualify for at least eight o'clock shadow, wrinkled jeans, messy hair and they were standing in the middle of a small village at the top of the world.

Why did she feel like she was home?

Everything about this situation and about him should have been unfamiliar and strange.

But it felt right, the weight of his arms around her and the way her head fit against his shoulder.

The hug went past friendly but she couldn't let go. There was no feeling of brotherly love, either. Just two people resting against each other.

She should step back. And she would, in a minute.

A loud whistle must have brought Daniel back to his senses because he immediately backed away. Instead of brushing it off, pretending that it had been a friendly gesture, Stephanie braved a glance at his face.

The wrinkle of disgust he'd worn when she'd asked him out on a date was missing. So was the fraternal long-suffering she'd seen growing up. Now he studied her face carefully, the surprise changing to his normal, serious expression. He cleared his throat. "Guess I better get to work." He waved toward a small building with a tiny bench. "Kids are in school. We'll be inside doing wellness checks and vaccinations, dental checks. Yell if you…have any trouble." Then he trotted over to join Dr. Weaver, apparently without giving her another thought.

She was tempted to stand there while replaying the feeling of being held against Daniel's chest.

But that would lead to heartbreak. He had a calling here in South America, while everyone she knew would agree that her place was safe within the bosom of Holly Heights, tying for Most Popular Teacher every year and wading through movie reviews that were supposed to be critical reports on literary classics.

For now she had a job to do. She picked up her camera and started exploring Plata.

The distraction kept her mind off the hug, her attraction to Daniel Lincoln and the reminder that what went up had to go back down. All the way back to the truck. A long, long way down.

CHAPTER SEVEN

AFTER HE SHOOK the hand of a little boy who'd refused to leave his mother's lap all afternoon, Daniel waved and then stretched his arms slowly to relieve some of the tension. He enjoyed talking with patients and his Spanish had become so good that he rarely needed Luis's help, but the smallest kids were always more challenging. Tears were hard, but screaming was enough to rattle him still.

Then he realized the room had emptied. Only Teresa was left, and she was gathering all the remaining supplies.

He hadn't seen or heard Stephanie since he'd run away from her like a coward.

Daniel wasn't sure what he expected to find after three hours of treating every school-aged child in Plata, as well as some of their parents, but he'd worked with one ear cocked for any noises coming from right outside. He hoped Stephanie had stayed out of trouble, but he'd been too busy to check.

He wasn't sure what to say to her.

On top of that the hug had confused him.

It wasn't the first time he'd wrapped his arms around Stephanie Yates. When she, Rebecca and Jen had been kids, he'd caught her more than one time as she flew at him.

But this time he hadn't wanted to let go. That hug had been celebration and congratulation and confirmation that she was all right.

"Good job packing, Teresa." His bag was lighter as he slung it over a shoulder.

"Anxious to check on your girlfriend?" Weaver asked as he sidled up next to Daniel, his own bag dangling from one hand. "How did you make her finish the trip? Taking her back would have been better. You wouldn't have a crick in your neck from checking over your shoulder all afternoon."

Daniel snapped his head around and bit back the angry words that would be hard to take back. Some of his anger must have shown on his face. Teasing was one thing, but criticizing his work was over the line. And Stephanie was off-limits either way.

Weaver held up both hands in surrender. "I'm teasing. Hey, no offense, man."

Daniel took a deep breath. "Couple things. She's not my girlfriend. She's an old friend who happens to have deep pockets. And I can't make her do anything. It's taken me some time to wrap my head around that, but I've got it. You'd better get that straight, too, unless you want her to prove it to you in some way that makes you both mad."

Then he turned and walked away before he added anything else.

Then he realized he'd meant every word. Stephanie Yates made up her own mind. She'd proven that again and again, this trip was just the latest example. In Holly Heights that might be harder to see, especially since she spent so much time doing things for other people. Here she was no different, but the change in scenery shone a bright light on what made that service possible. Determination. Smarts. And a strong will that kept her going even when she was scared.

He wondered if she understood she could do anything she wanted.

At some point he should figure out why hearing Stephanie referred to as his girlfriend had sent a flash of pleasure through his chest and then another wave of all-out panic.

The first he could blame on homesickness. Right? It had been more than two years since he'd been to Texas. When the summons for the fund-raising event had landed in his email inbox, he'd almost felt happiness at the promise of going back. Catching up with his baby sister in person would be nice.

But then he'd remembered the way his colleagues had shunned him. Instead of being the hotshot surgeon who was biding his time until he hit the bigger leagues, he was the guy who'd gone around the protocol, ignored a direct order from the hospital administration and had gotten into a shouting match in front of board members.

Then the program that would have benefited high school kids for years was canceled, and the impact of his bad decision spread beyond the hospital doors.

He'd done it all for the right reasons.

Or so he'd thought.

Then he'd insulted one of the few people in town who would have understood his motivations and urgency even if she could have charmed everyone into a better solution, one that served them all.

His own arrogance had led him astray. Twice. Each time he'd said exactly the wrong thing.

The patience he was learning here might have come in handy if he'd picked it up sooner.

Searching Plata wasn't a big job, but the round of giggles he could hear coming from outside the small school was a clue to Stephanie's whereabouts.

He wasn't surprised when he stepped into the small courtyard and saw her center stage, a boy and a girl on either side. "Good morning, Roberto. It is nice to meet you." She shook his hand and then repeated herself in terrible Spanish while all the kids sitting around her laughed. He wondered how many times she'd slaughtered the same phrase. Didn't matter. The crowd was still eating it up.

He crossed his arms over his chest, propped one shoulder against the wall, and watched her charm her volunteers and every kid in the courtyard. Even the principal had a smile on his face, and Daniel had never seen the man do anything other than frown.

She might be covered in dirt from her shiny blond hair to her fancy running shoes, but it didn't slow her down a bit. Stephanie was still the most popular teacher here.

When Weaver, Teresa and Nicole joined him in the audience, Stephanie started her final act. She named easily a dozen of the twenty or so children there, made outlandish guesses for the others to elicit peals of laughter and shook hands with the dour principal who hugged her neck. After a quick bow, she blew them a kiss and trotted toward the group as the kids told her goodbye and asked her to come back to see them.

"Sorry. One thing led to another…" Stephanie's voice trailed off as she reached around him to grab her backpack. "But I got some great pictures with permission from Senor

Martinez. Who is awesome, by the way. So generous. He invited me to dinner, but I didn't know if you guys normally eat here."

Weaver tilted his head to check with Daniel. "Don't think we've ever been invited."

"Somehow I doubt we were this time either," Daniel murmured and waved a hand at the kids who were all still waving.

"Weird," Stephanie said as she struggled to get the backpack on her shoulders. Before Daniel could help, Weaver had smoothed the strap over her shoulder. "Maybe there are too many of you together."

And maybe the principal had fallen under Stephanie's spell like everyone else.

It was good to know the man was human.

As she led the way out of town he could hear her chatting excitedly with Teresa and Nicole about all they'd managed to accomplish over the afternoon.

Apparently the altitude wasn't bothering her anymore.

"We should plug her in tomorrow. I can think of a few things she could do to help." Weaver held up both hands again. "But you're in charge. You call the shots.

Just thought I'd mention it." He hurried to catch up, and Daniel could hear him complimenting her on her way with kids. Stephanie laughed, but whatever she said slipped his mind when Weaver reached over to pat her back.

And in another surprising shot of emotion, jealousy wrinkled his brow.

They slowed to watch Luis navigate the steep steps, and Stephanie frowned and bit her lip.

"Here, I'll go first and help you down." Weaver turned around to negotiate the steps like a ladder, the perfect demonstration on how to get down. Teresa and Nicole traded skeptical looks. When Stephanie shrugged and started to follow, Daniel grabbed her hand.

"Let Teresa and Nicole show you how easy it is." Daniel motioned at them to get on with it. Teresa and Nicole traded another glance, and Daniel knew neither one of them was fooled. Weaver wouldn't be, either.

Apparently Stephanie was the only one who had no idea what was going on. She huffed out an impatient breath. "Okay, Dad, but it doesn't seem advanced. Like a ladder."

Dad? He was going to have to make it clear he didn't appreciate the nickname. Just as soon as he figured out why that teasing name annoyed him.

They bent over the side to watch Weaver, stuck in the role of gallant, helpfully guide both Nicole and Teresa down the last drop, the biggest step. Teresa nodded once and brushed his hands off her hips before Weaver turned and made a beckoning motion at Stephanie. "Let's go, beautiful."

Stephanie quickly stepped back from the edge, her eyes big and a slight turn of her lip showing her surprise. And possible disgust. She leaned closer. "Is he hitting on me? Here?" She smoothed a loose hank of dusty hair behind her ear. "Is he blind? Should a blind dentist be treating patients?"

Daniel shook his head. "Man's got a pretty good eye, I'd say. But if anyone will be helping you down, it's me." He took a loose strand of hair and rubbed it between his finger and thumb. "And when he calls you my girlfriend again, I'm going to agree.

Just so you don't fall off the mountain when it happens."

Weaver had his hands propped on his hips. "Step back," Daniel said. "We're coming down." He glanced over his shoulder to see Stephanie staring off in the distance as if she'd been frozen in place. "Hey. We're going. Climb down the ladder, like you said. I'll be a few steps below you so if you stumble, I'll catch you."

He waited for her to agree and slipped her backpack off her shoulder and on to his own. "This is easy. Gravity does most of the hard work. You can do it."

She narrowed her eyes at him, and he wondered if he should have stopped right before that. Encouraging her probably had less positive effect on her confidence and nerves than telling her she shouldn't do it.

If he'd tried that—telling her she shouldn't take a step without him—she'd already be down and halfway back to the truck.

He maneuvered his way down, a careful eye on Stephanie above him. She was covered in half the dirt in Peru, but she was strong and tall and beautiful. When he guided her down the last step, she fit against him like that was where she belonged.

Then she stepped back and raised her hand for a high five from everyone in the group.

Even him. That rankled a bit.

He wanted more than high fives. Maybe another hug. Or a quick kiss in celebration.

"All right. Achievement unlocked, and I didn't break my neck. Next up, walking a mile without dying." She took a deep breath and slipped into the straps of her backpack. "Slow and steady, people."

Stephanie, Teresa and Nicole started down the narrow path behind Luis. Weaver raised an eyebrow at him. Daniel ignored it and hurried to catch up. At the first sign Stephanie was in trouble, he would be the one to save her.

The trip back took twice as long as it normally did, and Stephanie applied a fresh layer of dirt after a short pit stop to catch her breath, but she made it.

And she did it without any help from him.

"Now then, should I ride in the bed of the truck?" she asked as she patted her jeans.

They all watched the dust surround her like a cloud. "If someone will kindly knock me out so I miss how the truck gets turned around, I would appreciate it."

He listened to them laugh and realized she had easily conquered this crowd, just like she had the schoolkids, just like she would any group she walked into because that was who she was. And all of a sudden, he resented it. A little. He wanted her to be awkward and shy just once.

"Everybody in. And close your eyes." He saw the little frown crease Stephanie's forehead and realized if she heard his gruff tone, so did everyone else. And he had no good answer for why his mood had changed.

Everyone was quiet as he made the difficult turn to get the truck headed back to town. Weaver refused to look in his direction. Stephanie caught his eye any time he checked the rearview mirror, but he had no answer for the question she was asking.

He didn't know what was wrong with him.

If he was working himself into a black cloud because of jealousy, he ought to throw himself over the side. He'd had a golden opportunity with Stephanie and he'd messed it up. Now they were worlds apart, literally, on most days. He had his work here. She had her whole life to lead with no restraint, no history to hold her down.

Eventually they made it back to Alto, and he took a deep breath as they unloaded. Space. That was all he needed.

"And now, I believe I'll go and take a shower, perhaps turn it into a mud bath," Stephanie said. "I hear it's good for the complexion. I'll be down to help with dinner, Teresa."

She paused on the stairs and studied him, her head tilted to the side. "Everything okay, D? No casualties after all today. That's a good thing, right?"

He forced a smile. "You did great." She rolled her eyes at him and walked slowly up the stairs.

She had. So had Teresa with packing the bags. Nicole and Weaver had managed all their patients without assistance. And Stephanie had conquered a town.

Nobody had needed him.

It was a lowering realization. Other people were good at their jobs, too. He didn't hold the success of this venture in his hands. If he hadn't been there today, they'd have managed quite well without him.

Daniel had to wonder what he was accomplishing with his time in Peru. Was he making amends or just…hiding here?

STEPHANIE CLOSED THE door to the women's dorm and collapsed against it with a muffled groan. Faking cheerful energy had been a bigger challenge than walking to Plata. Now all she wanted to do was stretch out on her bed.

That was it. Lie down and ignore the dust cloud following her. She had no idea what she'd do once she made it there. She could sleep. Possibly she'd take deep, satisfying breaths in and out and celebrate not dying in the dirt on the side of a mountain.

Or she could remember leaning against Daniel, talking to Daniel, getting a glimpse of the real Daniel, turning the images over and over in her mind until she convinced herself those were just some nice moments between friends.

Because at this point she was finding it much easier to remember the crush of uncomfortable, unreturned emotions and the embarrassment of stepping out on a limb only to fall flat on her face.

So she should definitely not drop face-first on the bed.

The dust cloud that would result might cover the entire room like volcanic ash anyway.

Bending down to untie her shoes was also out of the question. She toed them off, one arm braced against the wall for balance, and then stumbled into the tiny bathroom, whimpering the whole way.

"Wash my clothes first? Or get the dirt and creepy crawlies out of my hair?" She studied the contraption over the shower-head to determine whether or not chancing an electrical short was worth hot water. The small window at the top of the shower stall should definitely be closed before she turned on the icy water, but the idea of stretching her arms that far reminded her of the way she'd felt staring up the steps to Plata. "Or maybe wash my clothes and me at the same time. Efficiency." Her clothes might insulate her against the shock of freezing mountain water.

She stepped under the heavy spray and managed not to yelp with the shock of icy needles hitting the top of her head. "Everyone does this. You can, too." She gritted her teeth and wiped the fall of wet hair out of her eyes to study the muddy rivers running down into the drain. Getting out of wet jeans might finish her off, but at least the clothes they'd bury her in would be clean.

Frozen stiff but clean.

After what felt like hours—but had to be seconds or her nose would've frozen completely off—she squirted shampoo in her hand, closed her eyes and used unknown energy stores to wash her long hair.

When she eased her head back to rinse out the soap, she opened her eyes to see the world's ugliest lizard staring at her from the shower wall. Honestly, it had to have been an alien lizard: creepy peach-colored skin and flat black eyes watched her as if it was studying where to launch its first attack.

If her muscles hadn't already been frozen in the pain and shock of cold water, she might have made a run for it. Instead, all she could do was yell. "Help! No, really, somebody help!"

She'd never been able to put forth a satisfying scream, but when the lizard darted toward her instead of out the open window, she was gathering her breath to give it her best shot. The door to the bathroom opened, Daniel stumbled through and he yelled, "What is it? Are you hurt?"

Instead of answering, mainly because she couldn't, Stephanie pointed at the lizard, which seized its chance to up the creep factor by sticking out a long, black tongue. Daniel rubbed his forehead. "A lizard? Really?" He shut off the water, grabbed the lizard and dropped him outside the window before he slid the window closed.

"Hopping a plane to South America all by yourself is no problem. Charming a village of kids when you don't speak the language is easy. Even picking yourself up out of the dirt when you can't catch your breath you manage. But no lizards. That's where you draw the line?" Daniel laughed and shook his head. "And do I even want to know why you're standing in the shower fully clothed?"

His warm approval, the completely ridiculous situation and the remnants of fight-or-flight panic all combined to make Stephanie break out in uncontrollable giggles. When she leaned against the tiled wall with a solid squish, Daniel joined her, their laughter loud in the tiny space.

Eventually she caught her breath. "I was being efficient, washing my clothes and myself in one long river of mud. See?"

He frowned but nodded. "Okay, I might buy that."

"And you know I've never been good with slithery things. Remember that time we all went to Adventure City and Jen dared me to touch the boa constrictor?" The memory was enough to make her shiver. The icy water dripping from her hair didn't help.

"Yeah, I stayed way back. I was afraid she'd pick me next." His disgusted face nearly sent her over the edge into laughter again. "But a lizard's different than a snake."

She leaned forward. "You're telling me you didn't think that was one creepy lizard? You saw the black eyes, right? They matched his tongue." She widened her eyes to punctuate the horror of the moment.

"It's too bad we don't have a camera to capture this, to save it forever." Daniel picked up her wet hank of hair and squeezed water out in a steady trickle.

"No need. When you tell Jen and Rebecca, they'll laugh without any photographic evidence." Their eyes met and they were both grinning. "Thank you for saving me. Again."

He waved one hand and then shoved it in his pocket. "You would have saved yourself if you'd had to. Again."

She hoped he was right, but it was annoying and frustrating to realize she'd called out to him to save her. Any ground she might have captured by proving her mettle on the road to Plata had just been lost.

Lizards were the worst.

"I hope you're right. Doesn't change the

fact that I didn't have to, thanks to you. Maybe you need a cape."

"Tossing a lizard out an open window doesn't seem like much of a superpower." He wrinkled his nose. "Pretty lame."

He'd always done that, taken on the weight of the world without an understanding of how much it might mean. "All I know is, I'm glad you were with me on the path to Plata. And I appreciate you picking up the lizard so I don't have to."

She watched him frown. In his world, only the big gestures counted: saving a life, making a breakthrough, moving to a completely different world. He'd never understood how he helped every day.

"You're easy to count on, Daniel. You know that, right?"

"Until I meet a rule I don't like. Then all that goes out the window." He smiled. "Sort of like the lizard."

"To look at you striding down the halls of Holly Heights Hospital, I would have thought you knew exactly how much people respected you, depended on you." She shook her head sadly. "But you don't, do you?"

Their eyes met and locked. Every bit of air in the bathroom disappeared, and breathing became a challenge for the second time that day.

"Respect is one thing, but what about friendship?" One corner of his mouth turned up, but no smile showed in his eyes. "Especially after you make a mistake that leads to newspaper coverage and losing your job."

She wanted to tell him none of that mattered.

But of course it did. He'd worked hard to get where he'd been. And even a man who knew he was good at his job would have found it difficult to face off against that much disapproval.

How many times had she said yes when she'd wanted to say no to avoid the tiniest chance of disappointing someone?

"That would all change, you know. If you come home now you have volunteer service to be proud of in addition to the years you served Holly Heights." She shrugged. "And you still have friends. Jen, Rebecca and I have worked with the kids of most people in town. Don't underestimate our influence."

She waggled her eyebrows as though she was teasing, but there was some truth, too. "People have short memories, you know. Eventually you could…even get your job back." Maybe. She had no idea how that worked, if the administration could still keep him from practicing. But there were other hospitals. Not in town, but closer than Peru.

"People might have faulty memories, but I don't." He snorted. "And you can bet the hospital administrator wouldn't forget, either. But there are other hospitals. I could go home if I wanted."

So why didn't he? She inched closer to touch his shoulder, determined to find out what kept him here, but her feet slipped. He caught her, but instead of turning the near miss into the perfect kiss, worthy of a blockbuster romantic comedy, Daniel steadied her, patted her shoulder and left.

The bathroom door shut with a thud, and she caught a glimpse of herself in the mirror over the sink. Stringy wet hair. Mud trails down both sides of her face.

She wouldn't kiss her, either.

He'd been disgusted at the suggestion when she'd been spit polished.

Now? He'd seen her at her worst, her most ridiculous and covered in mud.

If she'd been subconsciously dreaming of changing his mind, she'd probably settled the issue for eternity. The lizard had a better chance of getting a kiss.

She turned on the icy water , gritted her teeth and stepped back under the spray. Friendship. That's what this whole trip was about, proving to him and now herself that they were always going to be good friends. He'd rescued her from the slithery thing. That was enough.

Then she'd move on to Paris, find a dark-eyed romantic to pour her red wine and forget this lizard had ever happened.

The fact that the man she imagined holding the wine carafe looked suspiciously like Daniel Lincoln in a beret was nothing more than fatigue. "Frostbite on my brain, that's all." Her teeth were chattering before the water ran out, but the mud river finally ran clear.

She hoped her brain caught up quickly.

CHAPTER EIGHT

AFTER HE MANAGED to escape the bathroom, Daniel trotted down the stairs and out the front door of the municipal building. He didn't slow until he was through town and standing at the top of the path he usually followed to the river.

If he had any retreats in Alto, this hike led to one, a quiet spot by the water. It wasn't an easy descent, but once he was there he had plenty of space to think. He propped his hands on his hips and studied the path before he took the first step. Focus mattered on this trail. One wrong step could lead to a long fall. If he survived, getting help would be difficult. He'd broken one of his own rules by leaving without letting someone know where he was going.

But he didn't want company.

And he sure didn't want to see Stephanie

before he had a chance to get the crazy urge to kiss her under control.

Even though she'd looked like a drowned mud pie he'd almost done it in the cramped bathroom.

Almost. But he'd remembered who he was and who she was and where they were in time.

She was his sister's best friend, and she'd been like a sister to him.

He had a strong feeling she would have been happy to kiss him back, too. What a temptation.

Hiking down, down, down and then fighting his way back up was the best solution at this point. The distance was easy; the elevation change was brutal. He followed the dirt path that meandered through rough brush and green pasture until he reached the small grove of apple trees that lined the river bank.

Before he sat under his favorite tree he turned back to stare up at Alto, the only sign that there were other people in this world. The town and the road marked a definite line on the mountainside. Above it was steep rock and dirt, a sheer wall that soared over the town. And below it, as the land dropped to the river, a gradually deepening green marked in squares by rough rock walls.

Carrying the corn and potatoes back up to Alto was a feat he couldn't even contemplate, but men, women and children did it daily.

He flopped down in the shade, wrung the water out of his shirt, courtesy of Stephanie's odd shower, and closed his eyes, ready to leave some of his burden here by the river.

Somehow, the complete silence broken by the trickle of water made it easier to think. Whether he was overwhelmed with the work that needed to be done or struggling with homesickness or caught in the regret loop that made it hard to sit still inside his skin, he could come here, sit, clear his mind.

Today all he could think of was Stephanie. Wet, bedraggled, tough, funny Stephanie.

And the way she had felt in his arms, her lips dangerously close.

The shock had nearly sent him down in a tangle with her except the bathroom was entirely too small for them both to fall. One of them would have hit the wall sooner or later.

He'd had to get out. Saying goodbye would have been the normal thing to do, but he hadn't had time for that.

"It's because we're here. If we were at home, kissing her would never occur to me." He covered his face with both hands and wondered who he was trying to convince. Just him and the birds and bees here.

He rubbed his forehead and squeezed his eyes shut. Birds and bees, that was always what it boiled down to.

Instead of wearing himself out by going in circles, he focused on the slow-moving water, the way his breath sounded and the feel of sunshine on his legs. Before he'd landed in Peru—beat up, bruised by his own mistakes and at the lowest point of his life— he'd have scoffed at the idea of meditation making a difference.

If anyone confronted him about his riverside escapes he still might, but being still, concentrating on his senses, and blocking out the fears and frustrations that made it difficult to focus on his job helped him face every new day.

If he'd tried this when he was a hotshot

surgeon who liked expensive cars and lots of praise, he'd have taken fewer risks. Most of them had paid off, but he'd never forget the one that hadn't.

Most days getting his head together was easy enough.

Today it took twice as long. A blonde beauty kept floating to the surface, and none of the reasons that kissing her was a terrible idea had changed.

Daniel felt a cool breeze, his warning that the sun was going down behind the mountains. He stood, stretched out the muscles that had become tense and glanced up at Alto.

The moon would be bright, but negotiating the path in the dark was a risk even he didn't want to take. Breaking a leg would mean a long, hard ride back to Lima.

And it might be hours before anyone found him in the first place to haul him up the mountain.

With a deep sigh, he started up the trail, welcoming the way his muscles burned and focusing on the air moving in and out of his lungs as the altitude increased.

When he made it to the road into Alto, he paused with his hands on his hips and concentrated on slowing his breathing, returning his pulse to normal.

Definitely not an excursion he'd be taking Stephanie on, not this time around.

At the thought, he cursed and kicked a rock over the ledge.

He'd gone on this hike to get his mind off of her. What a waste of time.

"Act like you've got your head screwed on straight then." He walked through the center of town and waved at the small group of musicians setting up around the dusty, dry fountain.

Teresa motioned him into the kitchen as soon as he stepped inside the municipal building. "Dinner's ready. I made chicken and potatoes. A meal like no one's mother used to make but pretty tasty here on the mountain."

He patted her shoulder and watched her smile then look away. "Thank you for saving us all from my cooking." He filled a plate and wedged himself in at the small table. "Where's Steph?"

"Stephanie is lying facedown on her bed. I can't tell if she's exhausted, mortified or both." Nicole poured water from the pitcher Teresa had filled. "You should go talk to her."

Daniel watched Teresa and Nicole trade glances and figured he was being set up. "Rest will do her good."

No one said anything else as they concentrated on their plates.

"Well, she's got to eat, Daniel," Weaver said from his spot in the corner. "I should fill her plate, take it up to her and keep her company for a bit." He fidgeted as though he was about to stand, and Daniel shot him his best arrogant glare. It had been a long time since he'd needed it, but he remembered how.

"No need. I've decided not to die of embarrassment," Stephanie said as she eased around Daniel and walked to the stove. "Sorry, Daniel. You're stuck with me a little longer."

Her clothes were dry. Her hair was getting there. The mud was gone. "Glad you came down. There's nothing to be embarrassed about."

She didn't answer, just looked away,

grabbed a cereal bowl and started filling it with the leftovers. Then she leaned against the counter and stared at her food so hard he wondered if she thought it might walk away. "There's going to be music tonight," he added. "You should go."

"We're all going. The band means the whole town will be there, so we'll have a volleyball game, too. I need Nicole and Stephanie on my team." Teresa tossed a towel at Stephanie who dodged it. "Nice agility. And the height will definitely help."

"Not according to my seventh grade PE teacher. Every window in the square will be in danger." Stephanie shook her fork at Teresa in warning. "I hope you can live with the consequences."

Teresa shrugged. "Sure. We've moved to a place with absolutely zero glass. It'll be okay. We may have to retrieve the ball when it lands inside a living room, but I imagine we can get away with that twice before the game is canceled."

"Too bad it's not a dart game," Daniel said. The urge to contribute something to the conversation was overwhelming. The fact that she wouldn't look at him made it doubly necessary to speak up. "Right, Stephanie?"

She nodded and shoveled more potatoes into her mouth.

He glanced around to see that everyone was staring at him. They were either sympathetic or confused or both. "She's good at darts."

"But I've never had a lot of luck with games with nets." Stephanie wrinkled her nose. "You may want to pass out helmets."

Weaver was shaking his head as he cleared the table. "This I have got to see. They may write ballads about the horrors of this match."

"Catch up with us, Stephanie? We'll get everything set up." Teresa pointed her finger at Daniel. "And you're coming this time. Got it?"

He saluted and waited for them to ease past him before he moved over to the sink. Stephanie took one of the empty seats to finish her dinner, her back firmly to him. He ran the water and started cleaning up the dinner dishes. Neither of them said much until she approached the sink to hand him her bowl. When she stepped close, he turned to look at her, dutifully ignoring the way his world had narrowed down to the two of them.

"Thank you for rescuing me," Stephanie said and smoothed her hair behind her ear. Just like that she was the young girl he'd known forever, but when she stared up at him through her lashes, he decided she was so much more. "Teresa's going to be disappointed. Remember trying to teach me a jump shot?"

He laughed, but it sounded rough and wrong. "Not that my jump shot was ever much to brag about." Then she wrapped her arm around his waist to lean against him like she used to do, and he pulled her closer with one arm around her shoulder. They stood there for a long second.

"Thank you for being such a good friend, D. This is a trip I'll never forget." Before he could figure out what to say to her, she was leaving. "Got to strap on my running shoes so I can make a quick getaway if needed." She winked at him and then disappeared.

Unsettled at the distance between them, Daniel thought about tracking her down and demanding to know what was wrong. He'd done the right thing. Could she tell that he'd been thinking of kissing her? Was she upset by that? If she was, he could try to convince her it had been a weird blip, an aberration brought on by their proximity. She might believe him.

What if she wasn't upset? What if she'd felt the same attraction? Could she forgive and forget and give him another chance? He wouldn't be as arrogantly dumb this time around.

He stared out the tiny window at the pasture behind the building where a donkey grazed contentedly.

This time around? Any involvement with Stephanie was an even worse idea this time around. They were separated by an ocean.

As he worked methodically through the dishes and put everything away, he was afraid he knew exactly what she meant about her trip being hard to forget.

Unfortunately, after she left he had the feeling he was going to spend more time thinking about Stephanie and home than he should.

BEING INCLUDED IN a volleyball game had been pretty low on Stephanie's list of worries. It should have been higher. Her skills were almost as rotten as she'd expected.

On her first serve Stephanie completely missed. The ball bounced harmlessly on the hard-packed dirt of the town square. The young girls seated in front of the fountain giggled, the sound echoing off the buildings. The musicians, who'd been playing before the match started, had set aside their guitars to watch the game. They'd pick back up their instruments soon. She hoped.

Stephanie tugged down the bottom of her T-shirt and swiped her ponytail back over her shoulder, just to pretend she'd meant to do exactly what she'd done: miss by a mile.

And then she noticed Daniel, one shoulder propped against the wall, a small smile on his face.

"I told you you'd regret this. Being tall doesn't mean I have any natural athletic talent." Stephanie glanced over at Teresa in time to watch the incredulous stare replaced by what was supposed to be a look of support.

"No problem. Try again. We've got all

night." Teresa didn't sound completely sincere, but Stephanie didn't blame her. Not much anyway.

Her second serve somehow went behind her own head to bounce down the road out of town. Both teams and all the spectators turned to watch it disappear.

"You really were not kidding, were you?" Teresa said, hands propped on her hips as they watched a group of boys run after the ball.

"Take me out, coach," Stephanie said as she ignored the flush of embarrassment. "That's right, isn't it? Instead of put me in. I want out."

"Good suggestion." Teresa pointed at a shy girl who had been keeping score. "*Por favor?*" She made a pleading motion with both hands. "Help?"

When everyone clapped and encouraged the girl to take Stephanie's place, Stephanie coaxed the girl into a high five, did a curtsy and then moved over to join the group of giggling girls.

And immediately wished she could remember more than how to ask where the library and bathroom were.

"Here. They love balloons." Daniel held out three balloons and started blowing up a fourth when she took them from him. He tied off the hot pink balloon, held it out to the smallest girl and smiled when she hesitantly accepted it.

After he wandered off the rest of the group burst into high-pitched laughter again and the ice was broken. Two little girls immediately stood up and started batting the balloon back in forth. They were in training to become master volleyball servers someday. She should have started much earlier.

"How are you?" Stephanie asked. Her halting Spanish must have been good enough because the boldest little girl, who was wearing a PAC-MAN T-shirt, answered for the group. "Very well. And you?"

Stephanie eased down beside them, more comfortable now that she'd opened up the conversation. This was going to be easier than she'd feared.

"Very well also." Stephanie stretched forward to bat the balloon back to the girls who were playing. From general conversation starters they moved on to whether or not

Daniel was her boyfriend. Or so she thought. She was pretty sure *novio* meant boyfriend.

She made the universal "boys are gross" face, pinched her nose between her fingers and shook her head. Whether or not they believed her, they all laughed. Three more girls jumped up to join the wannabe balloon volleyball team, leaving her with the youngest. They talked about their birthdays, favorite days, colors, months and numbers, all topics Stephanie could swing without a translator and perfect for the age group.

The music started again, mellow notes and words that were beautiful even though she couldn't understand them, and she and her new friends swayed along.

When the volleyball game ended in loud shouts of triumph from Teresa's team, Stephanie scanned the crowd to see Daniel seated on a curb across the square, Luis and another young guy next to him. Whatever they were discussing, it was serious.

Of course, this was Daniel. Catching him with a serious expression wasn't even a challenge. Even as a kid, she and Rebecca had worked hard to break his frown of either concentration or disapproval.

Sometimes she was sorry for all the time he'd wasted trying to keep them in line.

But now she wondered if anyone worked to lighten his load.

Teresa and Nicole joined the group of girls who'd worked through her supply of balloons after the first three met mysterious ends in loud pops. When the last one popped over the heads of some grandmothers and earned the whole group a stern talking-to, everyone dispersed. The band of musicians played one final song and families started wandering down the dark streets.

"What's the deal with the electricity?" Stephanie asked as she pointed at the single streetlight over the square and the yellow glow spilling from one open doorway. "Why isn't there more light?"

Teresa shrugged. "Not sure. During the day the electricity is spotty, but we always have it when we need it. Maybe it's a cost thing." She pointed at one couple who were walking away, their arms intertwined as the man whispered in the woman's ear.

"Or maybe they don't need electricity. You know?"

Stephanie took the hand Teresa offered to help her off the low curb she'd perched on.

"Glad to see you got the good doctor down here. Most of the time prying him from the planning or reporting or budgeting or whatever he does is harder than the hike to Plata. And you know that's hard."

"Anybody offer to help?" Stephanie bit her lip and tried to tell herself this was not her fight. Daniel was a grown man. He was head of these expeditions. Maybe there was no other option but for him to carry all the weight.

Or he did it because no one else would.

Teresa frowned. "Well, now that you mention it, probably not." She sighed. "He's nearly impossible to help, you know. You should have seen all the lobbying I had to do to take over the meals. How hard is that to let go of? I mean, nobody's going to die if I'm not a good cook. Get sick maybe, but we did have a doctor on hand. And if I can't do it, you don't let me try again. Easy." She waved her hands. "But no. First it was rotations with these complicated schedules. And let me tell you, I hate scrubbing the bathrooms. That made me mad, which made me dig in twice as hard until I finally won."

The picture was crystal clear. Daniel never had been easy to talk out of something, especially when he was caught up on what was "right" or "fair." He'd decided that sharing equally made the best sense, and he'd go down with that ship.

Sharing the load was an excellent inclination.

Grim-faced determination to do an equal share of every single job, whether he was good at it or enjoyed it, wasn't.

And neither was expecting himself to make every decision alone and perfectly perfect every single time.

Teresa sighed. "I should have learned from that and tried my best to help in other places. I see what you mean."

Amazed, Stephanie laughed. "Are you a mind reader? I didn't say that."

"No, but I could hear my mother's voice in my ear, reminding me that taking the easy way out is a disappointment almost every time." Teresa shook her head. "She's been gone five years, but some things are still as clear as the frown on your face."

Since she'd spent a lot of time imagining her own mother's disapproving face on the flight down to Peru, Stephanie understood how easy it would be to hear her mother's voice.

"I didn't mean to frown, I was just thinking, trying to come up with some way to help Daniel. That's all. And believe me, I understand exactly how hard that can be. Years of experience." And his sister had her own fair share of stubborn independence. Watching the two of them try to out-help each other had amused Stephanie more than once.

"Getting him out here was a big step," Teresa said. "Keep it up."

"Do you know who he's talking to? I mean, besides Luis?" Stephanie glanced over her shoulder to see Daniel shaking hands with the kid.

"Not really. He's studying at the high school, but I don't know his name." Teresa pointed. "That's the principal there." An animated man in a dark hat was clapping Daniel on the back and then shaking hands with the kid they were gathered around.

Stephanie waved at the last of the little girls. Her name wouldn't come but Stephanie thought her birthday might be in January and she was pretty sure her favorite color was pink.

Since that had been the top pick for favorite color, it was a safe guess.

"I'll go help Nicole with the equipment." Teresa held up one finger. "And then I'll see what other task I can wrestle from Daniel. Thanks for the reminder."

Stephanie was shaking her head because Teresa had taken a point she hadn't even been trying to make. It would help Daniel, so she decided to let it go.

"Good night?" Daniel asked as he walked slowly toward her, his hands jammed in his pockets. "The giggling was a big clue."

Determined to get them back on track, Stephanie waved her hand breezily. "Oh, you know, we were comparing our birthdays and favorite numbers. Like girls do."

She hated awkward distance between

them. Just because she'd been pretty sure she was begging for a kiss and he'd turned away again didn't mean she should change her plans. Good old friendship was still the goal.

He nodded before matching his steps to hers. "I'm glad you came down tonight. I didn't notice the flash of a camera though."

"Oh, no!" Stephanie smacked her forehead with one hand and grabbed his forearm with the other. "I completely forgot! I was… in the moment, I guess. I'm really sorry."

He shrugged and took her hand in his. "I'm sure we'll have plenty to work with. There'll be another chance before you go home." He tangled his fingers with hers and they walked slowly down the shadowy street. "And I want you to focus on our work, not our play anyway."

Instead of driving herself nuts about whether hand-holding was ever truly friendly, Stephanie said, "Well, being part of the community helps with the work, doesn't it? Gains trust."

"Sure. Usually I leave that part to the rest of the team." Daniel rubbed one hand through his messy hair. "I used to think it's better for the doctor to be a bit more…distant."

"For the doctor or the patient?"

When he didn't immediately answer, she wondered if she'd overstepped. This friendship business could be tricky. She wanted the best for him. His sister thought that meant coming home, but there was no way to deny how much good he was doing here.

"What's good for the doctor is good for the patient." He tilted his head. "How's that for dodging the question?"

"Hmm." She pointed over her shoulder. "Who was that you were talking to?"

"His name's Marco. The principal mentioned to me that he might like to study medicine." They paused at the steps to the municipal building. "After your suggestion about a way to increase the local medical staff, I asked to meet with him. And I've been thinking about adding a piece to your report, a fund-raising request for scholarship support."

"Yes!" She jammed both fists in the air as if she'd become the lightweight champion of the world. "I'm awesome. I can't hike. Or speak Spanish. Or vanquish ugly reptiles. But my ideas rock!" She trotted in a circle until he chuckled.

The warm satisfaction at being able to help him and make him laugh transformed her silly grin to a stinging tickle at the end of her nose.

As though she was going to tear up.

Daniel saved her. "Hold off on the celebration. First we have to get the money. Then we'll have to get the word out. And then we'll have to find medical students. It's not a slam dunk. Not yet. Mostly it's just a whole lot more work."

"But I'm in the air, the ball in my hand, right? I'm headed for dunk city. Is that a thing?" This would combine two things she was passionate about: education and helping these people get quality medical care.

She froze in her tracks. Education, yes. Medical care?

"Dunk city?" Daniel asked. "I don't think that's a thing. But it's frustrating that good medicine always comes back to money."

Daniel watched her carefully, probably

waiting on her to seize the opening to discuss his battle with Holly Heights Hospital.

But she wasn't up to a fight, not until she figured out how she felt about him, this place and her future.

"Yeah, ask a teacher about school budgets sometime. Money makes the world go around, but I happen to have a fairly good lead on funds that could get the scholarship program off the ground." She paced in a circle. "I'll take the translator, do an interview with Marco and the principal, maybe Marco's parents or teacher. Then we can calculate travel expenditures for the doctors you bring in and come up with a proposal for years of service in return for tuition." She stopped in front of him and waited for him to correct her, direct her, improve her idea.

"And I'll take another long, hard look at coming back to Texas to raise money. Dr. Wright insists I can double our fund-raising if I'm there in person, but—" he cleared his throat "—I'm not sure she's right. Or that I'm up to coming home."

"Oh, come on. You're braver than that. Look around you. If you can build this clinic, you can take a quick trip home, put on a beautiful suit and schmooze some bigwigs. If you really care, you can do it." She waited for him to argue or agree, her heart pounding. Rebecca would be thrilled to see him, if only for a visit.

Instead he stepped closer, pulled her against him and wrapped his arms around her. So instead of asking him a million questions, words that would put them back on the right path, she tangled her hands in his shirt, rested her forehead on his shoulder and leaned against him, content to wait right there for him to do the right thing, remember who they were.

"Thank you for everything, Steph. I don't know whether this will work or not, but your enthusiasm for the project…for every project is exactly the boost I needed. You're optimism wrapped up in a package of home." He ran his hands through her hair and rubbed small circles on her back while they stood there under the dark sky, the only light coming from the bright windows of the municipal building and the silvery moon and stars overhead.

She took a deep breath to savor his warmth

and the powerful connection between them. Then, before she could think better of it, she eased back and seized her chance. She pressed her lips against his, hoping he'd meet her halfway because walking out on the ledge all on her own made it nearly impossible to ignore how far she had to fall.

For a brief second his lips softened against hers, moving slowly while his hands slid up over her shoulders. As a teenager obsessed with romance, she'd imagined kissing Daniel Lincoln more than once. Those fantasies were nothing like this. Then she'd been certain he'd come rushing in to save her from whatever boring episode of her life she was currently enduring: study hall, dateless Saturday night or the worst homecoming dance with Tucker Hall, son of her dad's boss. And "My Heart Will Go On" would be playing in the background.

Instead, her running shoes were firmly planted on a rocky dirt road and the sounds around them came from a light breeze and a braying donkey. None of that mattered. She could stand here forever knowing they were together again.

Then he was easing back.

"Steph, this is a mistake. I ran like a scared jackrabbit earlier because I realized that. And not even the insane hike down to the river, my favorite spot to focus and get myself together, completely cleared my head. That's dangerous. For me and for these people I'm trying to help." His firm grip on her arms kept her from spinning away. "Friends. We're friends. That's all."

She'd known this might be his reaction. The pain was rough, but it was impossible to ignore. "Right. Of course. This afternoon you made it very clear that kisses were off-limits. I don't know what's wrong with me. All this atmosphere." She waved at the starry sky and the dark street and hoped he wouldn't call her on her lie.

"I'm in Peru. You're in Texas. And that's the way it should be, Steph." He ran a hand down her loose ponytail. At least she could hear regret in his voice. Before, he'd dismissed her. This time he seemed sorry the answer had to be no. "Doing this, working here, is possible because I'm certain Rebecca is happy, and I count on you and Jen to keep her safe and yourselves out of too much trouble. When I think of Holly Heights, I imagine the three of you camped out in my living room. If that ever changed because of something I did—like hurting you—I'd never forgive myself."

"You should come back, take over the managing of our lives," Stephanie said and hoped he thought she was teasing. "You're lucky Holly Heights is still standing without you."

He shook his head and took two steps away from her. "Even if I come back, it won't be to Holly Heights. You know that. I was fired. I'm too difficult."

"But there's still Austin or…" Stephanie realized she sounded like a child who'd been told she couldn't have a puppy for Christmas.

"I'm exactly the right kind of difficult for this place. You can see that." Daniel nodded and waited for her to do the same. "And you're absolutely perfect for Holly Heights."

The reminder that Daniel, like Jen and Rebecca, her mother, the other teachers, and nearly everyone who'd lived in town since birth, couldn't imagine that she might be perfect somewhere else was discouraging.

Disappointing.

Maybe she should forget the lottery winnings, her dreams of escaping and…settle. Could that many people who knew and loved her be wrong about what was best for her?

"Okay. Sorry. I just…the atmosphere." Stephanie crossed her arms over her chest and leaned against the rock wall that marked the edge of the street. Wishing Daniel far, far away was a sort of new experience, but she gave it her best shot.

Still he didn't leave. Before she could figure out how to make it clear his presence was unwanted without sounding like a brokenhearted girl, he said, "I can't leave you out here, Steph. Let's go inside."

Instead of kicking her feet in the dust, she sighed. "Right. Rules. Safety. Following orders. Maybe I'll give that a try." Even she could hear the disappointment in her voice. She hated that.

"Big brother," she muttered. Stephanie eased around Daniel, trotted up the steps and disappeared inside before he caught up. When she was safely alone behind the door to the room she shared with the other women, she rested her head against it and closed her eyes.

Somehow, overnight, she had to figure out a way to pretend everything was normal. He was right. She wasn't planning to stay here and he wasn't planning to come home. Rebecca would always be her best friend, but bad feelings between her and Daniel might cause a strain neither one of them deserved. He didn't need any more burdens, and she had a feeling seeing her cast down over his rejection would be something Daniel would take personally. She could handle it in a grown-up manner.

Or she could at least fake it. Rebecca would see through her in a second, but Daniel could still be fooled.

With enough time, her lie that she was happy being Daniel's friend and nothing more, would become the truth.

CHAPTER NINE

DANIEL WASN'T SURE what to expect the next morning. After spending a long night replaying the kiss in his head while considering all the ways in which Stephanie was wrong for him but still so hard to resist, he was too tired to dance around the issue.

Skipping breakfast was no option, though he'd considered that during the early morning hours. Energy bars would work, but going without caffeine was a terrible plan. They'd landed in one of the few places on the planet without a coffee shop on every corner. Unfortunately, the size of the kitchen made it impossible to miss her.

Stephanie saved him again, of course. "What's on the schedule today, boss?" she asked as she slid a plate on the table in front of him with a steaming cup of coffee. Her impersonal smile would have fit perfectly on a friendly waitress. All that was missing was the order pad.

"Today we're here in Alto, over at the elementary school." He sipped his coffee and watched everyone nod in satisfaction. "We'll do school vaccinations and preliminary dental checkups. No walk-ins. An easy day. The clinic next week will be for new patients."

Teresa sighed. "And it's a good thing. My spectacular serves last night have left me with some muscle tenderness and a general ouch in my mobility. What do you recommend, Doctor?"

"Either find a fountain of youth or try ibuprofen. That's all I've got." Some of the tension across his chest eased as everyone chuckled and Stephanie joined in. "You okay?"

Stephanie finally met his stare, and the tension in the room doubled.

The absolute silence as everyone studied him and Stephanie was uncomfortable.

"Any pain from the hike yesterday?" he asked. "Or the lizard. Your two volleyball serves should never be mentioned again." Daniel bent his head to study his breakfast.

"Too true, but I'm fit for duty. There might be an occasional whimper, but we'll call it a quiet cheer for the team." Stephanie stood up quickly and groaned. "I didn't mean to do it that soon, but now we all know what's going on with my sore legs and we can move on." She picked up the empty plates, dumped them in the water and, instead of hanging around to help, headed for the door. "I'll grab my backpack and meet you outside."

Daniel watched her retreat, then felt like road kill as Teresa and Nicole raised eyebrows at him. "Guess you're on your own with the dishes." Teresa gestured to Nicole. "We'll pack the bags. We're here in town, so if we forget anything we can hustle back."

"You won't forget anything." He waved a hand. "But I do appreciate your taking that task over. I need to review my notes from last month and we'll walk over to the school. Weaver, if you have a minute, the principal has a student who's interested in medical school. I told him you'd talk with him about what it's like to be a dentist, particularly here on the mountain. Okay?"

Weaver nodded. "Sure. Be happy to." He

tilted his head to the side. "Wonder if there are any other kids like him. Maybe we should do some in-school talks about why we chose medicine. All of us."

The missing piece of his scholarship program fell into place just like that: mentorship. If they wanted to hire local doctors, first they had to build them. And fully staffed clinics and solid medical care required more than doctors alone. Nurses and office staff to keep the clinics stocked and fully operational would also be needed. Before he could do anything else like fund the unknown medical students, they had to find the kids with not only an aptitude but also the right kind of attitude.

His sister had been the first person to suggest a mentoring program. In Holly Heights. The one he'd fought to get approved by hospital administration and then torpedoed spectacularly.

He'd have to give it another shot.

"Great idea. I'll talk it over with the principals to see what sort of programs we might build."

Weaver held out his hand. "That's you,

Daniel. Never satisfied with the way things are. Always improving, aren't you?"

Daniel shook his hand although the "never satisfied" hit a sore spot in his ego. He was still puzzling over how that could be such a huge problem in his life when Stephanie came back in to refill her water bottle.

And instead of saying something sunny or funny or even acknowledging his existence, she turned on one heel before the water cooler blurbed its last bubble.

"Silent treatment?" He wiped his hands and tossed the towel over the drying dishes. When he'd first started, he'd been pretty sure dishpan hands were a real threat for a surgeon like him.

Daniel had set broken bones here in Alto. Sometimes he'd assisted with difficult births. Once he'd even removed an appendix under extreme circumstances. But surgery was a scary proposition here. Curing infections and soothing anxious mothers was the real job.

"Nope, deep in thought." She met his stare and the corners of her lips turned up, but her expression lacked the warm glow he'd always taken for granted. "What did you need?"

Disappointed that this might not be as easy as he'd hoped, Daniel said, "A teacher. I need a teacher's help. Weaver mentioned that it might be a good idea to do some programs in the schools, presentations or…" He shoved a hand through his hair, frustrated because he could see the seed of a great plan, but he wasn't quite sure how to grow it. "Something to get kids interested in medicine as a career. We need to identify kids with the skills, but even before that, we've got to plant the idea. Not only doctors but nurses, too. Maybe more. I'm not sure."

Stephanie stared up at the ceiling as she considered his answer. "Fifteen or twenty minutes at the beginning of the day with the kids, something fun. A mentoring program where high school students shadow you, assist with keeping records or…something. Possibly support materials for the science teachers." She twirled her water bottle. "I can help. You get me the introductions to the educators, loan me the translator and follow my lead."

He nodded. "Listen, I know you're upset and I should have never—"

"Upset, sure, but you don't understand why." She banged the water bottle against the table, but at least she didn't storm off. "After a long night, I realized what your problem is."

This should be interesting. Daniel propped one hip against the counter and immediately felt water soak through his jeans. "I have a problem?"

Her strangled response was more gurgle than laugh. "When I have the spare time I'll make you a list. But your problem, my problem, our problem is that you can't see me as a woman. I'm a woman, D, not a teenager who needs you to babysit. And I... I can make my own decisions. Even live with my mistakes, okay? Don't you think one minute longer about that kiss or even the mistake I made in asking you out, because I won't."

"What if I can't stop thinking about it?" He balled up the soggy dishtowel. "And you're wrong. I do see you. On this trip I've seen a brave, independent woman with talent. The school program? No teenager would be able to pull that off, but you'll do an amazing job."

Stephanie rested one hand on the water bottle and considered his answer. "Fine. I thought if you realized you don't have to protect me anymore, we could be equals. And if we're equals, there's nothing holding us back from…whatever."

She blinked at him and he understood her reluctance to fill in the blank. Would it be love or heartache? Either way, everything would change.

"Nothing except an ocean and the different lives we're going to lead." He crossed his arms over his chest to ease some of the ache that bloomed there at the thought.

She shook her head. "How is it possible that you, of all people, don't understand that people change, lives can change? With the right incentive, that change can even be the best thing that ever happened."

She left before he could explain that this was his place now.

Coming to Peru had given him a chance to start over. Living here might not be easy, but he knew what to expect and how to make a difference.

She was all about home and Holly Heights.

Whatever they could build together, they'd have to go home. And he'd have to face his mistakes and the people who'd witnessed them firsthand. Why did that feel so scary?

And when had roughing it in Alto become the safe choice?

"You ready?" Weaver stuck his head in the kitchen. "The bags are loaded."

Impatient with his own thoughts and second-guessing himself—a luxury few doctors had time for—he nodded. "Yeah. Let me grab my notes."

When Dr. Weaver fell in beside her, leaving Daniel and Luis in the lead and Teresa and Nicole chatting up ahead, Stephanie wasn't sure what to think. After her discussion with Daniel, she could have used some time alone to get herself together.

On her way downstairs that morning, she'd planned to pretend everything was fine. Normal. But a night of replaying the kiss had done little to improve her mood.

And then instead of going along with her plan, Daniel had pressed his luck.

She wasn't sorry she'd given him a tiny piece of her mind. In fact, now she could think of so many other things she should have, could have, would have said.

Her labored breathing made her realize she'd picked up speed, her angry march closing the distance between her and the rest of the group.

"Beautiful day." Dr. Weaver smiled at her. "But they all are, at least until the rainy season, or so I hear. If you slow down a bit you can enjoy the scenery."

Stephanie did her best to ignore the flush of embarrassment at being teased about her near stampede.

"You haven't been here during the rainy season, Dr. Weaver?" She tried to picture what would happen to the roads. Would the mountain's sheer face become a waterfall? And were the streets muddy bogs? She pictured daily downpours, but maybe it was light showers. As dry as these mountains were any precipitation could be called a rainy day. Would spending time in Alto be as pleasant during the rainy days?

She'd pulled ahead of Dr. Weaver again, distracted by her own thoughts, when he slowed her down with one hand on her arm. As she glanced up to see his teasing expression, she understood a little better what her dating problem was. Here was a handsome doctor who'd tried to get closer the day before, and instead of making sparkling conversation, she was building a weather report in her head.

How sad.

And she couldn't even blame that distraction on Daniel.

"Please, call me Jeff. Unless you're a patient. Then you better stick with the doctor part." He winked at her, and she had to carefully school her features not to show her surprise. Should she wink back? What was the proper response to encourage winkers?

Then she wondered if this was her chance to prove to Daniel she was absolutely okay without him. So she giggled like a maniac.

That hadn't been her intention, but when both Teresa and Nicole stared over their shoulders at her, she decided she should turn it down a notch.

"Since I'm pretty happy with my dentist, let's go with Jeff." She watched carefully to see if Daniel raised his head or turned around. He didn't.

"You'll have to do better to get his attention. At this point he's absolutely focused on his patients." Jeff raised his eyebrows as he waited for her answer.

"Which is a good quality in a doctor, I'm sure." She thought about protesting that she didn't know or care what Daniel was up to, but the look on Jeff's face made it clear he'd see right through whatever she said.

"Definitely. But did he tell you about my idea for the school programs? Don't you think doing career day talks to get kids interested in medicine is a solid plan?" He pointed. "Hey, you're a teacher. You'd be awesome at drawing up some plans for us."

"It's a great idea. I've already got a rough outline of a program. Daniel's going to set me up with the principal and maybe we can even get something started while I'm here. If not, I can draw up some plans and email them. Finding kids in these towns who want to study medicine could be the solution to the problems HealthyAmericas is focused on, and I want to help."

"Well, writing a big check is a help, too, you know," Jeff said and smiled at her. "And you can do that from the land of free Wi-Fi and restaurant takeout."

And she'd be safe and sound in her little bubble, learning to be happy with tying for Most Popular Teacher instead of calculating what it would take to win, gritting her teeth to teach poetry and settling for a nice man who inspired as much passion as warm socks. A nice family, a nice career and no surprises.

Stephanie took a deep breath and squared her shoulders. She was a rich woman now. The money could help change her life. That was why people spent precious cash on the lottery in the first place, right? The promise of being able to live their dreams. At the least she should be able to buy adventure.

Unless being stuck in a rut had nothing to do with money and everything to do with her.

If winning millions couldn't satisfy her, she had to take a harder look at her life.

What would make her energized by her work and excited about her life?

The sort of excitement she'd felt ever since spotting Daniel across the lobby.

In two days she'd already done things she would be proud of forever. How much more would two weeks bring?

"Have I lost you again? Admit it. You were daydreaming about the restaurant you'd visit for lunch if you were at home." Jeff shook his finger at her. "You can't fool me."

"You caught me." She pressed one hand to her warm cheek. When had she forgotten how to pay attention to a conversation? That was supposed to be one of the things she was best at.

"What brings you here? Why aren't you writing a big check yourself? You have to miss those comforts, too." Stephanie knew why Daniel was passionate about the place. It was his refuge. What attracted the rest of the doctors and nurses who put their lives on hold?

"Sometimes I just want to be a doctor, you know?" He shrugged. "My practice is my own and I love it, but man, it's a lot of not being a doctor. Most days I'm more a CEO and a coach and a therapist and an accountant and a hundred other things. Here, I talk to patients. I help patients. Daniel handles the rest. Besides that it's beautiful here, and I appreciate what I have when I get back home." He sighed. "It's kind of like the perfect vacation. Except for the cold water."

She frowned as she considered his answer. It made sense, but maybe he was downplaying the biggest incentive. No matter how great the vacation was, he was still working, still helping people. Surely that was the draw.

His lips were twitching when she glanced up at him. "And I'm also the kind of guy who can take every good deed and find a truly selfish motivation, so that's impressive."

Daniel turned to watch her and Jeff together. He frowned but didn't say anything. Instead he greeted one of the men he'd been talking with the night before.

"I do like knowing my time here matters. At home I'm kind of the necessary evil. Here people are grateful for what I do and that's a huge boost to my ego and to my love of the job. But I'll be headed home soon." Jeff winked. "And Austin's pretty close to Holly Heights."

Distracted by the thought that Daniel might want to discuss his plans for the school programs now with her and the principal, Stephanie nodded. She craned her neck to see if Daniel was searching for her, but Jeff put a hand on her shoulder.

"That was a vague way of asking if you'd like to go out to dinner sometime. Vague usually works, and it saves me from crushing disappointment." He brushed imaginary dust off both shoulders. "I am a doctor. Mothers love me." He bent down to murmur, "And of the two of us I'm the one who fits the rest of your life. I still have the adventurous spirit, but you'll never have to live through the rainy season here. I'm like the best of both worlds."

Stephanie had to study his face for a minute to catch up on the conversation. "Dinner? You and me." She frowned. "Really?"

"Good thing I have a pretty solid ego. Otherwise that might hurt." Jeff shifted the strap of his bag and scanned the town to make sure no one was watching them. "But it's not like he's even asking, is it?"

"Ouch." The sharp pain that pinched right in the middle of her chest made her wonder if Jeff had been watching her epic fail at a romantic kiss under the stars. "There's nothing between us. We're friends. And I'd be happy to go to dinner with you sometime. Just… I don't know, maybe turn down your overwhelming charm. Right now it's blinding."

He squeezed his eyes shut and huffed out a laugh. "Yeah. My charm's a real problem. But my ego takes up most of the room."

Stephanie rolled her eyes. "Sure. That part's easy to see." She reached into her backpack and pulled out her journal to rip out a page. After she scribbled down her phone number, she handed it to him. "Call me when you're back. If I haven't jetted off for Europe or been buried under summer reads book reports, I'll be happy to share a pizza with you."

Then something clicked. This was how it happened. This was how every solid prospect turned into the kind of friend who sent her an invitation to his destination wedding. Why did she do that? Every date became a casual thing, like something friends would set up.

The men she dated were only following her lead.

Instead of treating each new guy as the possible hero to her heroine, she immediately made herself the easygoing best friend. Why?

She studied the way Jeff folded the page with her number and shoved it in his front pocket. Pizza and Jeff would be so safe. There was no risk. So how much reward could there be?

"Scratch that. Plan something nice. Expensive. I want a wine list and suit jacket required. Then call me." If she expected more, she might get more. Still, she didn't feel one bit of nerves or anticipation at the idea.

Jeff shook his head. "Too late. I can already tell you're more a pizza and beer girl than valet and tie required." He shrugged. "That's why I like you."

"If you two are done making your dinner plans, we need to sit down with Senor

Hernandez to discuss what sort of programs might work." Daniel's grim expression revealed nothing.

Except disapproval.

That she picked up on easily.

"Certainly." She marched behind Daniel and shook hands with the principal. Then they all crammed into his cluttered office.

From her seat in the corner Stephanie said, "Senor Hernandez, I'm not certain what Daniel's told you, but I have some experience in building lesson plans and teaching high school students. Right now, I believe the easiest way for us to get this program up and running is to pick a day where Daniel can bring in his team. After a short description of the jobs they do and the people they work with, one of them would do a short science experiment, something fun. Then—"

"We can iron out the specifics before our first meeting. Would you have the time, no more than an hour, probably less, for such a program?" Daniel's interruption shocked her so badly that Stephanie lost track of the conversation.

A short while later Daniel agreed to write

up a short proposal that the principal could discuss with his teaching staff. He made the universal writing motion at Stephanie so she got the impression that she'd be the one doing the drafting.

She was the one with the training and skill here. Why had she been interrupted, talked over and generally disrespected?

She could feel the tightness in her jaw and forced herself to loosen up. He gave orders. It was his way.

Watching Jeff transition from flirting to business was a revelation. The way Jeff deferred to her as the educational expert boosted her pride and her outlook.

She was good at her job. As far as she knew, Daniel had never been voted Most Popular anything.

"Want to help me with the kids while Nicole and I do exams?" Jeff asked as they stepped into the courtyard. "You could use some distraction. Or Daniel could. Might keep you from murdering him."

Daniel didn't say anything to her. "Teresa, let's head for the clinic." He didn't slow down to see if Teresa followed, probably because he was already behind schedule or something. That was fine. She wouldn't forget to pick this up later.

But apparently she was on her own, so she turned to Jeff. "Sure. What can I do?" If Daniel couldn't be bothered to give her direction, she'd make her own way.

Jeff took the pack Nicole had carried in. "Toothbrushes. Toothpaste. Every time we visit we do a short how-to. Easy." Jeff frowned. "Wait. Show me your teeth."

Stephanie sighed. "Worst pickup line ever." She opened her mouth in a big fake grin.

"Really? After the way I asked you to dinner?" Jeff patted her shoulder. "You're hired."

Before she could ask any questions or argue with him, Jeff and Nicole headed for the same building Daniel had disappeared inside.

"Fine. On-the-job training. The best kind." And it would help her ignore the seed of misgiving about handing Weaver her number. Already they were chummier than potential romantic partners should be. He'd seen her covered head to toe in dirt.

That was more information than he needed at this point.

At least he hadn't been the one to rescue her from the lizard. All romantic potential was squashed once a man saw her with mud rivers down the sides of her face.

Then there was Daniel and his obvious disapproval.

Not that it mattered. She was free to date whomever she wanted because Daniel had removed himself from the picture.

That and he was an arrogant jerk. She shouldn't waste another thought on him.

Except to outline all the ways in which he was an arrogant jerk. That would be her gift to mankind.

He'd made his opinion clear, and Weaver was exactly the kind of man he'd told her she needed: one who called Texas home and still picked up his mail there. The fact that Daniel was so comfortable giving her orders should have been her first warning sign— Arrogant Jerk Ahead.

She would finish the trip. Then she would go home, but not because Daniel ordered her to.

Mainly because it seemed like her one option.

Would heading back to Holly Heights like everyone expected be settling?

What about going out for pizza and beer with Weaver?

All she could picture was a rousing evening of shouting at whatever team was on the big screens at Caps, the Heights' most popular bar. Then he'd bring her home and try to kiss her good-night. She'd be weirded out at the thought of kissing the guy who'd given her a high five over whatever victory they watched. He'd settle for a handshake.

And she'd have another friend.

The fact that he'd asked her to call him Jeff and in her brain he was already Weaver, the name his colleagues and friends called him, confirmed her suspicion. It was difficult to spin romantic ideals around a man she thought of by his last name.

The one man in the world who was already a friend and kissed like she'd imagined…he didn't settle. He wouldn't.

When she saw Luis stick his head through the doorframe as if he was searching for her, she realized she was doing her best impression of a statue there in the school courtyard. "We can call it She Never Learns," Stephanie muttered to herself. Daniel was out of the question. Weaver was a problem for much later.

Now was for dentistry.

She squared her shoulders and marched into the small room where a group of ten kids waited along with Luis. If she had to guess, she'd say first grade. Perfect.

She'd worked her way through college at two different day care centers. These were her people. At the high school level she had to know the right shows and songs.

But at this age? Silly acts killed with kids this young. If she wanted their attention all she had to do was forget her worries and entertain. The timing couldn't have been better.

"Does anyone know the alphabet?" All ten hands shot up even before Luis had a chance to translate her question. "Perfect. I need one volunteer to sing and another to demonstrate." Every head turned to Luis. He smiled as he translated. And nine hands shot up. The tenth belonged to a little girl who quickly stepped behind two others who were jumping up and down. That reminded her of the way she and Jen had always wanted to be first, out in front, and Rebecca had done her best to fade into the background.

She kept an eye on the little girl as she called all three to the front. "Now then…" She reached into the bag and pulled out a toothbrush and tube of toothpaste and watched every eye in the room lock on to them as though she was holding a hundred dollar bill. "Can you guys sing the alphabet for me twice?" She held up two fingers. "I will brush and show you the proper dance." Then she waved her hands. "Then we will all dance together."

As soon as the little girls started reciting the alphabet, Stephanie did her campiest ballet while she also brushed her teeth. It was a real workout, but the giggles drew a lot of attention. Just before she switched to the next group, Daniel stuck his head around the corner, catching her midpirouette and frothing slightly at the mouth. His frown slowly faded, and he shook his head before he disappeared.

When it was time to hand out toothbrushes and toothpaste to the last group through, Stephanie wondered how much toothpaste it would take to overdose on fluoride. Still, it had been a good day. She'd lost count of the number of kids who would have sparkling teeth, but she'd taken plenty of pictures and had a few stories to tell. And while she'd laughed along with her students, the spark of an idea had started to form. She needed to add a video to the fund-raising request. The pictures would be adorable, but the sound of laughter and happy little kids singing would open hearts and checkbooks. It had to. There would be no resisting.

Even better than the new idea, she also remembered how much she loved working with eager students. Stephanie was reminded of Weaver's words about the boost he got from his patients here.

To distract herself from the question of what it would take to love her old job again, she considered the video piece from a few different angles. Her own travel blog could benefit from some video. Taping a short portion of the drive up, complete with the thumps and her squeaks of horror, would convey the remoteness of the villages more than still shots would.

She was studying her camera's video function while she waited for the rest of the group to finish up. Adding a video to the donor call was the first priority. She stared off into the distance as she tried to come up with someone she could rope into editing video for her.

"Good work today." She jerked as Daniel spoke. He was so close she should have heard him approach. "They loved you. That's no surprise. Your dance moves, on the other hand…"

He waited for her to laugh.

She cleared her throat instead.

"Thank you. I'm always a big hit with the young kids. Sorry we were so noisy." She shoved her camera in her backpack, ready to head out. If she stood here for long she'd explain to him how little she appreciated his attitude. Loudly.

"No, it was great. I like to hear the laughter. Reminds me why we're all here."

"Does it? Oh, you mean all of you." She made a dramatic wave. "Not me. I'm here to take notes." She mimicked his scribbling motions.

Daniel crossed his arms over his chest. "Somehow I get the feeling you're upset."

"Nope. I'm annoyed." Stephanie crossed her arms over her chest and squared off against him.

He cleared his throat. "Oh, about last night. Or this morning, I guess? Well, I—"

"Wrong again." She took a deep breath. "You need help. I'm happy to give it. But don't push me to the background or treat me as...your errand girl when you need my expertise. I'm a teacher. I speak the language of teachers, Daniel. You should have let me take the lead. No one, not Weaver, not Senor Hernandez, sees me as a kid who needs to stand quietly in the corner. Just you."

Instead of immediately shutting her down or giving her a haughty explanation, Daniel ran a hand through his hair. Then he met her glare directly. "It's habit. This is my project, my clinic, my plans, my place. Believing someone else could do something better than I can isn't always easy, but you're right about the meeting with the principal. I have an expert here. I should have relied on you more. I'm sorry."

She opened her mouth to argue but she couldn't figure out what to take issue with. "Well, okay." She shrugged for punctuation. "Good."

His lips were twitching as he added, "You really told me, Ms. Yates."

She shifted the bag on her shoulder. "You got off lucky."

"I hope, no matter what happens between us, you'll always tell me what you think, Steph. I depend on you." His face was serious, and she had the feeling the dumb kiss was behind them. She also knew neither one of them wanted to talk about it anymore.

Daniel glanced over his shoulder as Weaver, Nicole and Teresa stepped out of the small building. "I wanted to warn you about Weaver. He's…" He rubbed his forehead. "Be careful, okay?"

"Is he a cheater? What's with the serious face?" Stephanie forced a laugh. "Besides, he's going to turn into a friend, too. You all do." She studied his face and waited for his reaction, but Teresa led the group closer. "Want to help me, Steph? I'm in the mood for…fried chicken tonight. Could use a sous chef."

"Sure." She had so much more to say to Daniel, but none of it needed an audience. He'd apologized. Being angry with him would hurt her. He wanted to protect her like a big brother, not like the man she'd been dreaming of for too many years.

That man was out there. But she might have to leave Holly Heights to find him.

CHAPTER TEN

THE ANGRY SWAY of Stephanie's long ponytail was almost hypnotic, but Daniel snapped to attention when Weaver punched him in the shoulder. "Good day today. Got a lot of patients in and your girl Steph was a big help. She's good with kids."

"Yeah. Teacher." Daniel could hear the caveman grunt in his voice but decided he liked the effect. He wasn't all that happy with himself. When she'd snapped at him about respecting her expertise, he'd felt exactly like one of her students. Being schooled unexpectedly was never easy, but her point had been impossible to ignore. This learning to step back and trust other people to take the lead was something that required practice. At least he was certain she'd give him another chance to do better. Even before she'd become a teacher, she'd been big on learning from mistakes.

He'd also never intended to make her madder with his unrequested advice about Weaver. Didn't she realize he was only looking out for her?

No matter where he went or how far away she was, he would always do his best to make sure she was safe. That was his job. As a friend.

Instead of following Teresa and Stephanie inside, he turned to face Weaver. "Her name is Stephanie. And she is special. Remember that."

The slow grin that spread across Weaver's face made Daniel shift uneasily from side to side. It was the sort of expression a hungry cat might give a dumb mouse. There wasn't a lot of entertainment in Alto. Stirring up some extra drama would liven things up.

"She's just a friend, though." Weaver nodded. "Right? So, you have no claim. Why so territorial?"

Instead of immediately agreeing as they both expected him to, Daniel crossed his arms over his chest and studied his dusty boots.

"A friend who lives far, far away," Weaver added. "Some lucky guy who lives closer to home should have a shot."

"Far away? In my hometown, the place where my sister lives. Somehow that doesn't seem far away to me." Daniel glanced up. "The same sister who's been Stephanie's best friend since before they could drive." He should know. He'd been forced to act as driving instructor on countless trips to school and back.

That had to be where he'd learned to love a small taste of danger.

"So she's more like a sister, then. Even better." Weaver pulled up his phone and entered something that looked like Stephanie's number from the piece of paper she'd handed him before Daniel could stop her.

Daniel thought about explaining that friends didn't date each other's sisters.

But he realized it would bother him less if Weaver was intent on calling Rebecca instead. He was a good guy. Anyone who'd give up precious time to volunteer so far away from home had his heart in the right place.

Basically, if Daniel couldn't have Stephanie seated across from him on a date, he didn't want anyone to. And wasn't that an eye-opening discovery.

As he'd expected, she'd messed up his head.

"Wonder if I could convince her to stay in Lima an extra two weeks. When my tour is up we could see the sights together." Weaver winked. "And while I won't treat her like a sister, I'll make sure she doesn't regret it." Then he raised both eyebrows as if he was waiting for something.

The only answer that came to mind was a growl. Doing the right thing was a struggle sometimes.

Eventually Daniel said, "Good." Before Weaver could wind back up to whatever his ultimate goal was, Daniel dumped his bag on Weaver's shoulder and walked away.

Punching a member of his team would be worse than arguing with the hospital administrator in front of a full boardroom. And if he was fired from HealthyAmericas, practicing medicine would lose all its attraction.

Instead of heading to the river, Daniel started walking on the road above the town.

When he'd burned off enough annoyance, he eased down on the side of the road to stare out over the shadow of the deep valley.

Thinking of Weaver and Stephanie in a nice restaurant shouldn't be this irritating. Before she'd popped up in his corner of the world he'd done a good job of not thinking about her or home any more than he could help. Right now, he could see her across the table in Sala Italiana, but it wasn't Weaver across from her. How he got there, even in his imagination, was concerning.

The thought of going home excited him and scared him in equal parts.

Neither changed the fact that he had work to do here. He was the only one who could do it, too.

At least at this point.

Dissatisfied with his silly irritation, Daniel turned back to town and met the student interested in medicine. "*Hola, como estas*, Marco?" They shook hands, and Marco pulled out the brochures he'd mentioned for the university in Lima, where he was dreaming of studying.

As they talked, Daniel realized he could

further his plans by meeting with current medical students. Determining the best incentive to draw doctors would be the challenge. Speaking with them directly would help.

When the single light in the town square came on, Marco made his apologies because he'd promised to be home before dark. Daniel was still waving when the young man disappeared in the shadowed street.

"I SOUND LIKE such a nag, but the leftovers are in the oven," Teresa said when he closed the door to the municipal building behind him.

"Nah, nagging would be telling me how hard you slaved for such little appreciation." Daniel ran a hand through his hair and tried not to focus on how tired he was. "And believe me, I do appreciate you."

"I know." Teresa motioned at the stack of files slanting toward the wall. "I hope it's okay, but I picked through your files to update them on our visits this week. After you have a chance to review everything I've added I'll refile them." She patted the top of the ugly tower. "Paperwork is my favorite."

Daniel snorted. "Right. Said no one ever."

Teresa grimaced. "Oh, okay, so now I'm the nerd because I like forms. Thanks, boss."

Daniel pulled a plate out of the oven. "Sorry. I thought you were being ironic. My voice would have had a sarcastic bite if I'd said the same thing." He bit into the flaky chicken and closed his eyes to savor it. "How much would it take for you to stay here forever, Teresa? I have no fortune, but I'll get one just to keep you here. You're the best nurse I've ever met, and fried chicken like this…" He shook his head and took another bite.

"Wait until you see my penmanship. It's nearly an art form, if I do say so myself." She dropped another file on top of the stack. "And as far as staying here, you have to get the rules changed. Tours are no longer than three months, thanks to the visa restrictions, and once every year, according to Healthy-Americas. I'm not sure how you managed a permanent station, but there might be others willing to do the same. People like me." She tapped her chest. "And then you could take some time off."

He'd managed to convert his worker's visa to a residency through a lot of help from the staff at HealthyAmericas and some assistance from the Peruvian health ministry. Even with all those people working together, it hadn't been easy. "You know there's a lot more to it than getting me to say okay, Teresa." He sighed. "I'd never let you leave, given the choice."

She watched him devour his meal and shook her head when he checked the refrigerator to make sure there were no more leftovers. "You got it all, and Stephanie handled the cleanup. She's handy to have around. Fits right in."

Uneasy with the turn in conversation, he nodded. "She does. You think Weaver's a good guy? I mean, with women. He's obviously a good dentist."

Teresa pursed her lips and turned her head to study him as though he was a troublesome specimen under a microscope. "Stephanie's as good a judge of character as I am, Daniel. Plus, she's fully adult at this point. And not your sister. You have no say in her choices."

He started to argue, but it was impossible

to stare her down, so he washed his plate instead. "Right. Well, since you're doing all the work I was going to do, I think I'll…" Honestly, he had no idea. "Maybe I'll draft a letter for the head of the national university in Lima. Marco mentioned a kid from Alto who was studying medicine. There could be a chance for some residency or training programs here."

"Scholarships in exchange for service. Here." She tapped one finger on the table. "Smart. And don't forget the letter you're going to send Dr. Wright, the one that will make the case to extend my service indefinitely." Her lips were tight as she smiled. She wasn't joking. This mattered a lot.

Daniel crossed his arms over his chest. "I know why I'm here. Why are you? And why plan to stay?"

Teresa leaned back in her chair with a sigh. "You know that feeling where everything fits? I have it here. I've had it since my first tour and leaving, that's when I start to feel anxious. When I'm away, I worry. When I'm here, I'm happy."

"What about home? Don't you miss it?"

He hoped the question didn't make it crystal clear how much he missed home now and then. But that was normal. It had been too long since he'd been back to Texas. Things had gotten easier in Alto and in Lima, but Holly Heights would always have something he couldn't find here on the mountain: his sister, his home, his family.

"Sometimes. But when I'm home I miss here more." Teresa fiddled with the edge of the folder in her hand. "Don't you?"

He didn't know. He'd been convinced the way to do this properly was to fully commit, to make this his new home.

"Besides, sometimes things change so much that the best way to deal is to find some new scenery. When my mother died I thought the whole world should be as radically different as mine was. Here, away from home, this different setting feels normal. I feel like I fit. And when I'm home, the places that should be so familiar aren't. Something's missing. And the problem isn't so much the place, but because I'm different. You understand that, right?" Teresa asked.

He did. When he'd packed his bags the

first time, he'd needed to find a new place where he didn't feel so out of step.

This place and the work had been exactly what he needed.

Teresa hummed as she sifted through the stack of patient files, a small smile on her face.

"Thanks for working on the files. I don't know why I never asked for your help before." He picked up the top file and flipped it open to see shockingly good handwriting. "You're hired."

"Don't forget the letter, Daniel. You could take a month off, head home." She shrugged. "You're important. Never doubt that, but the systems you've set up could be carried out easily enough with the right help."

Her point was impossible to miss. And it was a good one.

In fact, Gaby was already proving that to be true in Manzana. With the right help from local doctors, both towns could have permanent and good medical care.

"I'll consider it." He slid the stack of files she'd already finished off the table. "I'll take these with me. Some light reading." Instead of trotting up the stairs to the men's dorm, he picked up a chair and carried it out to sit in the open doorway. As he scanned Teresa's notes, he was impressed with her thoroughness and initiative.

If only it hadn't taken nearly three complete tours for her to wrestle this paperwork away from him. He would have been able to do…something else for a long time.

And she deserved his thanks.

After all the files were stacked next to his foot, he stretched in the chair and stared up at the dark sky.

Adjusting to Alto after Stephanie was gone would be a challenge.

He couldn't lose Teresa, too.

Weaver was snoring like a hibernating bear when he made it up to the dorm, but he quietly opened his laptop and started a rambling letter about Teresa, her skills and her ability to lead her own team. Then he recommended the creation of a salaried position for team leaders like her.

Coming up with a way to fund those team leaders? That was another thing altogether. He reviewed the growing list of changes he was recommending, all of them united by one common factor: they would cost money he didn't have. The third time he grumbled out loud, Weaver muttered in his sleep so Daniel closed the laptop and decided that was a problem for a new day.

AFTER A LONG day and night of stewing, Stephanie had finally gotten a solid grip on her annoyance.

He'd apologized for pushing her into the background, so that was easy to let go. He didn't have the right to warn her about Weaver, but Daniel Lincoln trying to boss her around was nothing new. There was no reason to be upset.

She'd do what she wanted to do as she always had.

And he'd be too far away to do anything about it.

"All right. Another tough day. We're headed up to Cochas." Daniel cleared the table. "Teresa, you've got the bags. I'll finish these, and we'll hit the road."

When he didn't even look her direction, Stephanie steeled her nerve, cleared her throat and said, "And no one has to tell me to stay here this time." She waved graciously around the table. "You're all welcome."

"You made it to Plata. This hike is shorter. I have faith in you." Weaver winked at her and then wrapped his arm around her shoulder to give it a squeeze. If she hadn't been watching Daniel closely, she'd have missed the way his lips tightened in response.

She shrugged, happy when Weaver's arm slid right back off. "Thanks, but I have some ideas I'd like to get started on. I'll stay here and work. When you're back I may ask Luis if he'll help me get some information from the principal and the teachers."

Instead of sleeping, she'd spent most of the night staring at the bottom of the top bunk. Thinking about Daniel had made her angry. Wondering how Jen and Rebecca were doing back in Holly Heights had made her sad. The best thing to do was make a plan of attack. So that was what she'd done.

"The clock's ticking. I need to get my job done!" She eased around Teresa and guided Daniel away from the sink. "You guys get on with the day, and I'll show you what I've done when you get back. You are going to be so impressed."

Instead of arguing with her about coming along, Daniel dried his hands on the towel and studied her face.

Or she thought he did. She didn't look up.

When he bent down to murmur in her ear, it took every bit of willpower she had not to shiver.

"I really don't want to leave you here alone, Steph. You'll be safer if you stick with us."

Stephanie swallowed and took a deep breath. "You aren't going to order me along? Did you turn over a new leaf at some point?"

He was frowning when she managed to turn her head, but she couldn't stand to be that close to him for too long. Even with his latest set down, she wanted to kiss him again.

The struggle to let her make her own decision was clear on his face.

It was kind of cute to watch a bossy take-charge super doctor waffle like that.

So she patted his shoulder. "No worries. I'll work here until the electricity goes. Then

I'll take my camera out to get some good filler shots. I won't leave town."

"I wish you spoke Spanish." He propped his hands on his hips. "If this is to avoid me, then…"

"Are you kidding me? I have plans. Inspiration." She waved her hands vaguely around her head like a windstorm was brewing. "Can't let them get away. And I do speak some Spanish. I can ask where the library and bathroom are. What else do I need?"

"I have something else I could use your help with. Later. We'll talk about it later, okay?" His almost smile was nice, a good sign that he was okay even if she was still having to clench the countertop with both hands to keep from turning back to him. Or socking him in the arm. The way she felt, she could go either way.

Putting an ocean between them again might be the only thing that cured that.

"Sure. I'll knock out the rest of the list, boss. Please leave your laptop," she muttered. Stephanie waited for him to answer, but when she turned around, he was already gone.

"All right. Get to work." After the dishes were dry, she noticed Daniel had left his laptop on the table. Probably while she'd been singing "Natural Woman" into the suds.

She picked up her camera and notebook to head outside into the sunshine.

After all her photos were downloaded on to Daniel's computer, she flipped through the slideshow to see how many shots she'd taken of happy children. Whether they were chasing balloons or waiting in line for shots or dancing weird ballet to the alphabet song, every single child wore a bright white smile. Rosy cheeks, dark eyes, and a mix of school uniforms and cartoon T-shirts from more than ten years ago blended together to make a picture of such happiness.

She'd never have been able to imagine these kids or those laughs.

And now she'd never forget them.

Comparing these faces to the next crop of juniors who'd suffer through American literature and do their best to skate by made her remember how much she used to love teaching.

Before she'd settled.

When she'd first started, she was going to ignite a love of reading and critical thinking in each class she was lucky enough to stand in front of.

Now she embraced the countdown to the summer break. Just like her class did. Yes, her students liked her, but she wasn't sure she was changing lives.

"Education. That's the key. Here and in Holly Heights." No matter what, she still believed that. While she was here she would do what she could to help these kids get the education they needed. Healthy bodies and happy smiles were critical for every child.

And when she wasn't here…?

"I won't forget. There's plenty to do. I can…" She wasn't exactly sure what she could do from Texas, but there had to be something. Maybe another organization like HealthyAmericas used educators. "Or… is there a way to connect teachers with HealthyAmericas?"

She jotted a note to ask Daniel about the possibility of educational trips, summer camps or something, where science and math teachers traveled with them for a week or two. "In the summer. It's like a match made in heaven." The fist pump she gave might not have been strictly professional, but her audience was made up of two shy toddlers. Both were watching her from a doorway across the narrow dirt road. So she waved, watched their eyes widen, and then they darted back inside.

"All right. Fund-raising first." For the next couple of hours she sorted photos and started a simple layout with a description of one day's clinic in Alto. She paused on the photo Daniel had taken of her at the top of the stairs in Plata. Her goofy pose made her shake her head, but the fact that she looked so proud of herself was something to think about. She'd felt more alive that afternoon than she had in a long time. "Surviving death by extreme altitude will have that effect."

She saved that photo to the desktop, made a copy in a thumb drive, and finished writing up the list of things they'd accomplished for the town in a single day. If Daniel had the information, she was going to add how much the vaccinations cost and some statistics about the incidence of childhood disease and mortality.

She didn't speak statistics at all, but an internet search might help her find the right numbers.

After a check of the time and the status of the electricity, she decided to try for an internet connection. Her inability to speak Spanish might make this a bigger challenge than she was prepared for. But as she walked down Alto's main street she spotted a store displaying a sign that read Internet…not to mention the glass bottles bearing the red-and-white Coca-Cola logo.

"Hola!" The cheer in her voice seemed to startle the small woman behind the counter so Stephanie decided to turn it down a little. "Coca-Cola…" She frowned as she tried to remember how to ask how much something cost.

"Dos soles," the woman said and held out her hand. As soon as Stephanie dropped the money on her palm, her hand disappeared behind the counter and she whipped down a glass Coca-Cola bottle.

Taking a shot, Stephanie pointed at the laptop crammed in the corner. *"Y el internet?"*

Whatever it cost, Stephanie would pay. She wanted some news from home. After this long, even the junk email would be fun to delete.

The woman tilted her head to the side and studied Stephanie carefully. She wasn't sure whether the shopkeeper had witnessed her embarrassing attempt at volleyball—and if she had, whether that would help her or hurt her—but she was going to maintain her cheerful smile.

Murdering Spanish would only get her so far.

Eventually the tiny woman returned the favor, white teeth flashing as she waved her hands. *"Nada."* She motioned effusively toward the computer and around the empty store. Stephanie raised her Coke in a broad salute, said *"muchas gracias"* and slid down in the folding chair.

Wishing she could ask for guidance, Stephanie took a satisfying drink of the Coke. It hadn't been refrigerated but after so many days without any Coke at all, it still tasted like a dream.

"Maybe the formula's different here," she murmured as she studied the bottle. Then she tried to figure out how they managed Coca-Cola deliveries or deliveries at all on these roads and decided it must be her lucky day.

It turned out that getting on the internet in the mountains of Peru was pretty much the same as it was in Holly Heights. Stephanie hummed "It's a Small World" as she logged on to her email account. She uploaded the Plata victory photo and typed an email to Rebecca and Jen. After she typed "Photographic evidence so get ready to pay up" in the subject line, she wrote a few quick sentences about how much fun she was having with the kids and referred them to the blog she'd set up before she left town.

"'Thousands of Words and Miles.' It's a good title. A little long but…" She glanced over her shoulder at the woman, who was staring fixedly at her, and wondered whether talking to herself was acceptable Peruvian conduct.

The lights flickered above her, so she logged into her blog, the one with a single photo: her, perched on top of the piles of luggage she'd packed to bring to Peru. She looked happy, maybe nervous. And clean. So very clean.

"My kingdom for hot water," she murmured. She picked three photos from the memory card. The first showed the shadowy valley below Alto. The second was of the kids gathered around Daniel before the clinic started. And the third was her victorious pose in Plata.

She wrote up her encounter with the Andean wildlife in the form of the world's creepiest lizard, placed the photos and posted her second blog post ever.

Now that she'd spent a week in the Andes, she could understand that her travels would have so much more impact than expanding her own experience. Her friends could see the world, too.

As she shut down her internet session, the lights flickered again and then went out. When she glanced over her shoulder, the small woman shrugged in the international symbol of "What are you gonna do?"

Stephanie was laughing as she pulled out more money. "Coca-Cola, *por favor*." Drinking two sodas in the space of an hour probably seemed wildly extravagant to the woman who whipped out her hand to take the cash, but Stephanie was pretty sure she was running at dangerously low levels of both sugar and caffeine.

She slid the empty bottle across the counter, took a fresh bottle and stepped out into the afternoon sun as Daniel was trotting up the steps, his head down and his forehead wrinkled in a dark frown.

"Does an alarm go off when someone reaches for a second soda, Doctor?" she asked with a smile. He glanced up sharply and the frown transitioned into annoyance. "You made me believe Coke didn't come this far, but I would not be defeated."

"What happened to staying inside or sticking close?" he snapped.

"I didn't really expect you back this early." Confused by his temper when she'd pretty much obeyed the rules—this little shop wasn't that far—she turned the bottle slowly in her hand and waited for him to calm down. Then she said, "I'm sorry you were worried. I thought it was a good time to try sending an email to your sister and I've got this blog—"

"Leave a note next time." Daniel's shoulder brushed hers as he stepped around her and disappeared inside the store. Instead of following him to give him a loud piece of her mind, Stephanie counted to ten, walked slowly down the steps to the street and sipped her Coke.

Disappointment settled over her shoulders. Why wasn't he interested in her blog— the outlet that would hopefully change how she felt about being stuck in Holly Heights? Not even the cool-ish Coke could lift her spirits.

Before she made it back to the municipal building, he caught up with her. "And now the electricity's down." He didn't curse but she could hear it in his voice.

"I had nothing to do with it, Dr. Lincoln. I will testify to that in a court of law." She noticed he'd bought his own Coke and seemed to be concentrating on finishing it in one swallow. "Slow down, Hollow Leg. You aren't used to the good stuff."

She started to head up the steps to the front door because whatever his problem was, she did not want to get caught up in it, but he stopped her with one hand. "Follow me. I need to talk to you."

Instead of arguing with him over his words or his tone or anything to get herself out of another close encounter, she bit her tongue and followed. The surprised look on his face was satisfying before he turned and strode away, headed for the small, empty town square.

His long legs and irritation quickly put him in the lead. "We left early because I couldn't concentrate. And then, when I got here, I had to look all over for you because you didn't do as you promised. You should have stayed in the municipal building."

The anger and stress in his voice turned her confusion into guilt for a minute.

Until she remembered she hadn't done anything wrong.

And she wasn't going to trail behind him. She trotted to catch up and passed him in time to claim the shadiest bench. "Exactly how many places are there to look, Daniel?"

It was a small town. How much time could it have taken?

Apparently, it was the wrong tactic because his face turned redder. "More than you'd think. The road stretches on forever and on both sides there's nothing but a steep drop. All it would take is one wrong step. Don't pretend this isn't a big deal. I have to keep you safe. You have to keep your promises. That's it."

His fears made no sense. The first place she would've gone to find a visiting American would be the place with the comforts of home.

He was in no mood for logic.

And the only way she was prepared to talk about this without shouting back was to decide his concern for her was sweet. Also misguided, and he had a terrible way of showing it, but now was not the time to educate him on manners.

"I'm sorry for worrying you." Stephanie took a deep breath, hoping to give her own irritation time to evaporate. "But I did exactly as I said I would. I was fine. Happy here, doing the job I said I would. Take a seat. Take a breath. Everything is fine."

She waited patiently for him to slide on to the bench beside her.

"Are you humoring me?" He raised an eyebrow.

"Absolutely." She crossed one leg over the other, more at ease than she should be with a fuming, bossy male. They'd been here before. She could talk him out of it.

His reluctant smile confirmed it.

"The first draft of your fund-raising request is prepared. I'd like to add some statistics on the childhood diseases you vaccinate for and the impact here, if you have that information. We could add the cost, especially if it's low, to illustrate how much good any size donation can make."

"Yeah. Good. I have some stuff that can help." He stared hard at the road. Away from her. "And I'd like you to add some information on expansion, the possibility of recruiting doctors from the medical program in Lima and the plan to work with the schoolkids in the communities we serve.

Those are bigger ticket items, but the impact could last for generations."

He was right. This group of doctors could change lives in this area for generations.

Her nose started to sting and she had to blink back tears.

Being a part of that was unexpected.

And it might change her life, too.

Stephanie lived and worked less than five miles from where she'd grown up. She'd had the same best friends for more than a decade and it was hard to imagine anything changing in her own life. But maybe she could make it happen.

Then he said, "You shouldn't have come. This was such a mistake."

Stephanie's shoulders slumped forward. After all she'd done, his opinion of her hadn't changed. Instead of being a member of his team, she was a burden. Since she'd spent a day doing some good work for him, the unfairness was maddening. Unable to put the words together, she stood up to storm off.

All it took was his hand on hers to stop her in her tracks.

CHAPTER ELEVEN

DANIEL WAS AFRAID to let go of her hand because if he'd been in her place, he would have left himself here eating dust. Since he'd been frantically searching for her, a chance to catch his breath before she stormed off would be nice. That would take a firm grip. "Wait. Stop for a second."

She nodded. "It's a good thing you made sure to establish the rules, D. Otherwise, I'd be shocked at your bossiness."

"I was mad. I know why I was mad. My tone is what you object to?" He tugged her closer.

"Nope. At this moment in time, your personality is what I object to." She tried to free her hand but he held on.

"You said you'd stay close. You didn't. I've been worried about you all day and coming back to see that I had good reason…

Yeah, bringing you to Alto was a mistake, one that's starting to affect my work."

"That's on you, Daniel. I'm a grown woman. I make my own decisions all the time. I was perfectly safe. And if you'd been listening, I had my own project to work on." This time when she tugged her hand out of his, he let her go.

"Please, sit." He watched her closely and saw the instant when her sense of humor overrode her irritation.

"Did you say *please*?" She sat next to him and eased back. "This just got real."

He draped his arm along the back of the bench and stifled a grin. She'd never been intimidated by his temper.

Of the two of them, he was most surprised by his lack of control. Instead of the concern of a friend, he'd hit caveman levels of "mine" and "protect," as if he couldn't string together enough words and it didn't matter because she should already understand. She deserved better, but at this point he needed her company. Getting a grip would be easier since she'd punched a hole in his irritation.

"I'm your only help in this country. You

had no way to call me." He closed his eyes. All day long, he'd been imagining all the dangers she might stumble into. Treating patients while he was that distracted had been nearly impossible.

He tilted his head back to study the brilliant blue sky. There was not a single wisp of white clouds. In fact, the weather during the dry season was so superior to east Texas summers that he'd once used it to lure a pediatrician away from Houston for a month.

She rolled her eyes. "It's like you've somehow forgotten that I manage fine on my own, Daniel. Your sister grew up. So did I. We work and pay bills and date men, all without your disapproving frown scaring the less worthy away. And if you'd seen the last guy your sister met online, you'd know Weaver is a prime specimen, okay? We make mistakes and we fix them." She shrugged. "The same way you do."

"But you haven't done that in Peru. Here, you don't have a town full of people who'd kiss every boo-boo to make it better. This isn't Holly Heights." Daniel ran his hand down his thigh before he slapped some of the dirt off. He didn't have to wait for her correction for long.

"Boo-boo? Like I'm a baby?" She pointed at him. "That's what you think of me? After all this?"

He wanted to rewind the conversation.

He might even want to rewind the day. When they'd left that morning he hadn't been convinced leaving her behind was a good plan.

Now he knew it was the best test of how he'd feel when she was gone.

Lonely.

"Stop trying to big brother me back into the safe zone. All I want is to be the leading lady in my own life. But I'm only ever cast as the friend. The sympathetic shoulder to cry on, giver of solid advice and master of the witty comeback." She kicked a small pebble and they both watched the dust drift in the air. "All that's missing is the laugh track."

She crossed her arms over her chest, her long blond hair a silky trail down her shoulder.

"I need to focus on my job, Steph," he sighed. "And you should never be mad you make such a good friend. Seeing you in that lobby in Lima was a shot of encouragement. If we'd said hello and goodbye there, and shared a meal in between, then I would have been okay. Better than I have been in a long time. But having you here in my space, this place where I'm okay and doing good things, that'll make it hard to say goodbye. I'll remember you dancing with the kids, slaughtering perfectly good Spanish and…" He rubbed his forehead. "I can't get that kiss out of my head."

A bombshell like that ought to have been accompanied by a loud explosion.

This one came with heavy silence, as if the whole world was holding its breath to make sure time went on.

She stopped pacing and then the corners of her mouth twitched. "Like, in a good way, right? Not in a pitying, you should suggest a breath mint kind of way." She didn't step any closer but something changed between them. Her teasing set everything back in motion. The world didn't stop spinning because he admitted he might feel something for her other than friendship or responsibility.

Her shoulders relaxed and he realized she was the same girl who'd always worked so hard to encourage him.

"No, in the way you think obsessively about the person who can change your life." He wrinkled his nose in disgust. "If movies and books are to be trusted."

"I have to sit down. I can't catch my breath," she muttered and then dropped down beside him with a hard thump. "The most romantic thing a man ever says to me and it's you and it's here and…wow." She took a deep breath and stared up at the darkening sky.

He wanted to reach out to her. From here it would be so easy to wrap a hand over her shoulder and squeeze.

"You don't do things like other guys. That's for sure." Stephanie shook her head. "Normally, when I'm forced to sit through these talks I get to hear about how much my friendship means and how that's worth more than a romantic relationship. They start with the hammer and follow up with the cushion. Going from calling me a mistake to saying I might change your life seems a pretty big swing."

"Doesn't change anything. I belong here. You don't." Daniel moved his hand to avoid temptation. "I'll hate to see you go, but at least I'll be able to do the work I'm here to do without distraction."

Stephanie blinked and Daniel had the uneasy suspicion he'd gone too far. But then she straightened her shoulders. "You don't know that, Daniel. You tell yourself that. And you insist it's true, but you don't know me as well as you think you do. Not that I blame you. I'm not sure I knew me well before I got here. But I've realized that I've got to get out of Holly Heights."

"Sure. Fun trips to Paris. And Rome. Hawaii." He shook his head. "But you know you'll never leave, not for good."

"Well, one thing I know for sure. I'm not going to make a decision because I'm afraid. Not anymore. Can you say the same thing?"

Daniel studied the four little girls peeking at them from around the corner of the Alto store. He was trying to come up with an answer. "You think I'm afraid to go home?"

"Maybe. You ran. It all worked out, because the work you're doing here fits you.

I can't argue with that, and I'll be sure to tell your sister that you're happy and fulfilled and all good things." She heaved a sigh. "But… At some point, I have to face the truth. So do you. I'm attracted to you, even though you have a serious case of jerkitis sometimes. I would try to make us work, even separated by an ocean. Maybe you could consider for half a second whether or not you'd step foot back in Texas for me."

She crossed her legs with an angry jerk, and kicked one foot in a quick rhythm. "And not me from tenth grade. Me now. A woman."

When Stephanie glanced away, the girls watching them darted back behind the building, the trail of giggles the proof they'd been there. "We have an audience." She wrinkled her nose at him. "Your job matters. You can't make decisions on a whim. I get that. Here I've realized I need to do some serious thinking about what I want. You should, too."

"You're right. No whims. I wish I'd realized that sooner. Telling the hospital administrator he was a small-minded bigot with a calculator for a heart was ill-advised." He turned toward her. "Doing it in front of an audience of board members was nearly criminally insane."

He was afraid she'd leave him hanging, but she laughed reluctantly.

"Yeah, a little less whim would have been good there."

He finished the Coke he'd been gripping. "For the rest of the trip, let's—"

"What if...?" Stephanie cleared her throat. "I could extend my stay in Peru." She frowned. "Indefinitely. I mean, I work for fun now... If anyone does. Here I could try having fun for fun. Be a tourist, take day trips from Lima. See the sights. Do some of that with you when you have a day or two. Come along to help with the clinics now and then."

She barely looked at him. That was a good thing. He'd immediately started shaking his head, and he was pretty sure she would've taken it as another insult.

"There are people in my life who can't see the real me because they're so used to seeing what they want to see. The Stephanie who tap-danced in the elementary talent show, the girl who played Mary in the church's living Nativity for three years straight, the busiest reader on the Holly Heights pediatric ward, Most Popular Teacher. But that's not all that I am. I thought here I could be the braver, better me, but I can see that you're going to insist I stay in my spot, too." She nodded. "And I get that. It's safer when nothing changes. But not very exciting."

Instead of agreeing with her, he shook his head. Everything she mentioned reminded him of home, of all the things he missed now that he was so far away. How could being loved and protected be a bad thing?

Then he imagined what life would be like if he'd never come to Peru and he understood better.

"This is the most exciting thing I've done. I don't know whether I'm making a threat or a promise, but this won't be the last time I do something no one expects me to do." She smoothed her ponytail over one shoulder. "All my life, I've carefully navigated the small world of Holly Heights, but now that I know I can do something like hop on a plane and see new places, I'm not going to stop. I can't. I feel more alive here in this dusty little town than I have in a long time. And I don't want to lose that. I looked at you and saw this adventurer, but you aren't, are you? This is safe work in a safe place. You don't have to face disappointment or judgment. You're a hero here and nothing will change that."

The way she spoke made it sound like every word was dawning on her now.

And he'd been slowly working his way around to the same realization.

"But what about this friendship? It's special. And this place? How can I give it up?" He was starting to feel the annoyance again.

He'd have to decide if she was right later.

"Why are you so sure you'd lose either one?" She poked his arm. "It's because in your eyes I'm the sidekick. But I promise, I'm about to show everyone. I'm going to be the hero in my life."

She bent down and pressed a quick, sweet kiss against his lips before she hurried around the corner. Infectious laughter erupted when she found her target.

New town. Didn't speak the language. Stephanie still had a group of fans. As she led the group back into the small park area, Stephanie pulled a hot pink balloon out of her pocket. *"Rosado! Mi favorito!"* She rolled every *R* broadly and bowed when the girls clapped.

Leaving her here on her own had started this argument in the first place. But she didn't give him a second glance as she and the girls split into teams to bat the balloon back and forth. Stephanie made theatrical leaps to keep the balloon in the air.

And she didn't need him. At all. When she made it back to Holly Heights, she'd be fine without him. He had no doubt she'd make good on her promise to discover what she wanted.

He'd never been good at following rules when he didn't agree with them and staying inside the lines had sometimes chafed. That was why this assignment was perfect for him. If he didn't like the lines, he moved them.

Had Stephanie wanted to do the same? And if she had, how could she ever do that with the whole town watching? Of course coming to Peru had felt like freedom.

She was a friend, but what if she could be more? What if he could have everything—his job and a woman who made him stronger, better?

On the other hand, if she tried to make a life here and failed, neither one of them might find happiness again.

He might take the risk if he was betting only on his own future. He wouldn't gamble with hers.

Stephanie's balloon volleyball match was interrupted by loud honking from just outside the town limits. Around here, that could only mean one thing.

"Emergency. Everybody out of the road."

Stephanie pulled the little girls into a tight knot out of the way just as a small truck barreled down the road, heading for the municipal building. Daniel followed, running up the hill without another word, and Stephanie hurried after.

The truck skidded to a stop, the horn still blaring.

"Doctor." A young girl hurried toward Daniel. "There's been an accident."

She yanked open the door and a tall, thin man eased out, one hand wrapped over a bleeding gash in his side.

"What happened?" Daniel wrapped an arm around the man's shoulder and urged him inside the municipal building.

"Cusi was unloading a delivery. Everything shifted. His side was…" The girl closed her eyes as she tried to come up with the right word. "Pierced."

Blood loss was Daniel's first concern. Dark red covered Cusi's left side. If the wound was deep enough, he might not be able to stop the bleeding.

"Teresa," he shouted as he led Cusi to a chair.

"I'm here." She immediately started laying out everything he might need. His sterilized tools, local anesthetic, gauze, sutures, disinfectant—Teresa lined it all up efficiently while he eased up Cusi's bloody shirt.

And immediately he took a calming breath. "Pierce" hadn't been quite the right word. More like "a jagged tear" but that could be handled here.

Cusi wouldn't be bleeding to death today.

"All right, Cusi. First, we'll clean it. That won't be fun. Tell me all about what happened." He applied the anesthetic and started to probe the wound. As he worked, Daniel shut out the rest of the world. The blood flowing from Cusi's wound slowed. His focus narrowed to the wound and his hands cleaning and closing it.

After he tied the last stitch, he eased back on his knees, too tired to move out of the way. Cusi wiped tears on his shoulder and blew out a harsh breath.

"Step back, Daniel." Teresa nudged him aside and covered the wound with gauze. She described the antibiotic Daniel would prescribe, explained how to rebandage the wound and keep it dry, and listed all the dangerous signs to watch for in flawless Spanish.

Probably because she'd memorized it.

Daniel tried not to think about how much worse the blood loss could have been. He'd made them leave early today. He should have already met and helped Cusi at the clinic in Cochas instead of chasing Stephanie like an idiot.

This was almost his worst fear coming true.

He'd almost failed a patient. Luckily, Cusi had a driver and transportation. That was rare in the villages Daniel served. Without both of those, medical help would have been a long time coming, meaning more blood loss, increased chance of infection. If either passed the point of no return, Cusi's prognosis would have been much different.

All because Daniel had been too wrapped up in his personal issues to do his job properly.

A hand in front of his face snapped Daniel out of his thoughts.

Cusi grimaced as Daniel hauled himself off the floor and then shook his patient's hand.

"Gracias," Cusi murmured and held out a couple of nuevo soles.

Daniel took the money. "I'll see you in one week. Watch for infection." He nodded his head and waited for Cusi and his driver to agree. Then they were shuffling back out the door.

And he was completely done.

"Here. I'll make a note and add the cash to the envelope. Sit down before you fall down." Teresa patted his shoulder, took the money and eased him into a folding chair. "You've had a big day."

He noticed the blood on his gloves just before he rubbed his forehead. Then he saw Stephanie hovering on the steps to the dorms. Their eyes locked.

After a moment, she looked away and disappeared up the stairs.

CHAPTER TWELVE

FOR THE NEXT three days, Stephanie did her best to be the most productive and least noticeable member of the team. She battled with her guilty conscience, sometimes blaming herself for the fact that a patient in need had been forced to chase down the doctor. But it had been Daniel's decision to leave the clinic. No matter which side was winning, Stephanie understood Daniel's concerns after watching him respond to a real emergency. So, she washed dishes and took out the trash and kept her head down.

With Luis's help, she interviewed several students and teachers, asking about the benefits of science programs and how the HealthyAmericas team might assist the schools in expanding the curriculum and encouraging students to pursue medical careers.

And to be superhelpful she avoided any meaningful contact with Daniel. She didn't know whether to apologize or stick to her insistence that he should have trusted her to take care of herself. Instead, she left printed reports on his day's stack of medical files after each revision. At some point she was going to have to get some actual direction.

The long ride back to Lima would be soon enough. They'd need something to talk about besides their history and future or lack thereof.

She played another disastrous game of volleyball and managed to squeak in two more blog posts just before the electricity disappeared for the afternoon.

Reading the comments on her posts, written by her two best friends and her mother, was an exercise in patience. Every single one included some variation of "come home."

The latest email from her mother required even more patience.

It's time to start planning the Fourth of July fireworks show. I made sure to put you on the list for setup and cleanup.
Thanks, Mom

Stephanie swallowed the last of the Inca Kola as she closed her email. No questions about her work here. No comments on her photos or writing. Only a reminder that life went on in Holly Heights, and she'd be able to slide back in without missing a beat.

"Another?" The shop owner, who'd introduced herself as Tamaya on Stephanie's second visit, hovered behind Stephanie's right shoulder. She didn't speak a lot of English but they'd ironed out a routine.

"No. *Gracias*, Tamaya." She quickly paged down the blog to check for comments.

"Nice. Good picture." Tamaya pointed at a shot of Stephanie surrounded by her balloon volleyball team. How happy they all were.

She smiled over her shoulder, grateful for the feedback. More than once she'd almost asked for Daniel's opinion on what she was writing and posting.

But she hadn't and she congratulated herself on her willpower.

The thought that this would be the extent of her communication with him for the rest of forever—unless he came home—was depressing. But the alternative would've been worse. What if she'd convinced him to try for more and things hadn't worked out?

Daniel was right. He'd handled things badly, but this pain was bearable at least. Besides, he had a job. And the lottery had given her freedom.

"Whatcha doin'?" Teresa asked from the cramped doorway. Tamaya held out her hand, Teresa dropped money into it and accepted her drink with a happy sigh.

"Blog post. What do you think?" Stephanie leaned back so Teresa could read over her shoulder. "These are the pictures I asked your permission to take this morning." They'd given their first successful science presentation to a group of elementary school kids.

"I didn't know you were doing this. I'd love for someone to post daily photos while I'm stuck in Texas." Teresa frowned and reached over to scroll down. "Grinning like a seriously happy donkey, I am. Who knew I had that many teeth?" They both laughed.

"You're beaming. I love those pictures." She pointed at a photo showing the line of little girls gathered around a table. "Good job coming up with an experiment on such short notice. Maybe you should have been a teacher."

"No problem. I tried to reproduce one of my most memorable science moments." Teresa shrugged. "In first grade I had a teacher who loved to show how magic was just science. I remember being stunned at the way the candle behind the jar could be blown out. Air was mysterious, and I've always loved a good mystery."

Magic as science… Stephanie made a mental note to ask Daniel whether that might be a good hook for the donors, a way to tie everything together.

On the long ride back to Lima.

She should type up an agenda, a list of safe topics for the hours it would take to make it back to town.

Satisfied with her new posts and happy to have finished before the lights went out, Stephanie shut down her session. "Were you coming to use the computer? Need to check your email?"

"Nah, I was curious about what you were working on. Wondered if you were updating your online dating profile in preparation for your return home." Teresa studied her face and took a drink of the bright yellow Inca Kola. "It's like you're never around anymore."

"What do you mean? I'm always around! You'll all be so happy to get rid of me, I'm sure." Stephanie waved at Tamaya and stepped out into the sunshine. Her plan was to ignore the dating volley. No one was fooled about how she felt about Daniel. That didn't mean she wanted to spend any time dissecting it aloud.

"I'm trying to make sure I've got what I need to finish this report for Daniel. I can't believe that in two days I'll be back in Lima. I booked my flight home. It's crazy."

Teresa pursed her lips and didn't answer, just walked slowly beside her.

"I feel like I've accomplished some great things on this trip, but there's so much left to do. Maybe I finally understand how you feel. It's not easy leaving a job half finished. I'd be pretty anxious to come back if I were you." Stephanie wanted Teresa to agree. If one person would encourage her to take a bigger risk, she might find it easy to take another leap of faith.

Daniel wanted her to be safe in Holly Heights, and her mother would have patted his shoulder in wild approval.

Rebecca and Jen, the two people who knew her best in the world, agreed.

Was she being selfish to hope someone could take a minute to consider what she wanted for herself?

"I remember my first visit. A month seemed like forever when I was packing and trying to get things settled at home. But after that time was up, when I was faced with getting on the plane to go back to the daily grind, all of a sudden a month was not enough. It flew by. I still feel that way. In two weeks I'll be sad to be leaving and busy plotting my return."

The question that had been floating around in Stephanie's brain ever since her conversation with Daniel slipped out. "Could you just…stay?"

Teresa raised an eyebrow. "Are we talking about me? Or you?"

"I don't have any medical training. Why would I stay?" She tried for a carefree shrug.

She was happy here. And she could breathe here. And she was pretty sure that in Alto, the limits were due to resources, not expectations. But unless Daniel needed her here or wanted her here, there was no reason to exhaust herself trying to figure out a way to buy more time.

"Well, a certain doctor has special approval to stay through HealthyAmericas." Teresa wrapped an arm over Stephanie's shoulder. "Come on. There's gotta be something more than friendship. None of *my* friends have asked to come for a visit."

"I won the lottery. I wanted to make a donation."

"Sure. And all the rules say you have to hand the check directly to your intended recipient or that money flies away into the atmosphere. It's such a drag." Teresa sipped her drink. "Oh, and then you also have to cheat death on the side of a mountain, shower with local wildlife and help out with every single task. Those donations are work intensive. No wonder they're hard to come by."

Stephanie could feel her cheeks getting flushed. "Fine. I used to have a crush on Daniel. His sister, my best friend, has a photographic memory about this. She dared me to come here, and I couldn't refuse." It sounded ridiculous when she boiled it down like that.

"Or you didn't want to refuse." Teresa sighed. "And I get that. He's a great guy. I'm not sure he's 'put my life on hold, write a massive check, and risk life and limb' awesome, but there's no accounting for taste. I like guys who are more laid-back, but a lid for every pot and all that. Why didn't it occur to you that this might happen? That this crush might turn into something else? That he and this place together might be irresistible?"

"He'd already informed me once that it would never happen," Stephanie said and felt her lips twist in the same way his had as he'd told her that. And she'd remember the expression on his face for a long time, although now that she'd kissed him, his surprised response played right after it. And it felt good to be vindicated. A little, anyway.

"Ah. Okay." Teresa shook her finger. "Another time he was wrong, am I right? The guy's not nearly as infallible as he wishes. No wonder you like him so much, what with the bossiness and the inability to accept help like a normal person. Tell the truth. You think you can change him."

"Of course I can." Stephanie sighed. "Or if anyone can, it's me. And he deserves a little change. No matter the difficulties of his personality—and yes, they exist—he's a good man, strong, with enough honor to do the hard things without complaining."

Teresa tilted her head back to study the sky. "Well, when you put it that way it's hard to argue that he's not awesome. He's definitely the guy I'd trust to lead me on an adventure."

Stephanie shook her head, amused to hear someone else say what she'd always believed. He carried a lot of weight on his shoulders, mainly because people were so happy to hand it over to him.

She knew how that felt, only her burdens came from school functions and civic duty. After a while she'd wanted more.

But there, in the middle of Alto's dirt road, she wondered if she'd been trying to change the world herself, but in smaller ways.

Safer ways.

One volunteer opportunity or student mentoring appointment or encouraging smile at a time.

"What are we going to do?" Teresa leaned against the rock wall beside the steps that led to the municipal building. "Because if you leave and he stays, I won't get what I want, either."

Stephanie shifted her weight while she waited for Teresa to finish. "Which is?"

"I want to lead the teams here. Daniel's great, but he could move to the next area, set up another post. I could run the teams in Alto, continue his education focus and the mentoring program." Teresa turned to make sure she had Stephanie's attention. "I know I can do it here."

"Could you start a new program?" She tried to imagine Daniel leaving before he'd achieved his goals for the area and couldn't. Moving on to set up a new program somewhere else? That was easy to see.

"I'm not sure. I don't speak Spanish fluently. Not well enough to diagnose medical concerns. Here, I can get around. Luis is here. I know the people who speak some English if I'm ever in a pinch." She waved her hands. "Doesn't matter. HealthyAmericas would have to agree and there's the visa situation and all the red tape to work through to keep someone in the country on a permanent basis. It's a risk. Expensive. I understand why they don't want to take it."

"Could you talk to someone when you get home?" Stephanie hated to see Teresa's disappointment. She had a dream, and she was so close to getting it. "I'd be happy to write up a recommendation. And attach a check." She mimicked counting a big stack of money. Lightening things up seemed important at that point.

"A check, you say? And will you hand-deliver it so we know it counts?" Teresa smiled.

"Even better. I'll hand-deliver it to your new boss."

"Thanks, Stephanie. I've asked Daniel to recommend me as a permanent team member." She shrugged. "It seems important that he agree I'm needed here, and I know he's connected, being a friend of the founder and all. So, I'll work two more weeks, go home, pick up my Spanish lessons and wait until I can return. And it will all be okay."

Stephanie knew Teresa didn't mean what she'd said. The grim determination in her jaw was enough to convince Stephanie she needed to say something to Daniel. He needed help. Here was someone who wanted to do more. It made sense.

There was a solution to every obstacle Teresa mentioned. All it would take was some time and money to iron out things.

Well, and the effort of someone who cared.

Dr. Wright would be screening her phone calls by the second week Stephanie was back in Texas.

"Don't give up, Teresa. Remind him. Remember how you wore him down about dividing the chores?" Stephanie wasn't sure of all the answers at this point, but Daniel was the key to Teresa's success.

"Are you going to give up? Call whatever brought you to the Andes Mountains a silly crush?" Teresa tilted her head. "Being a quitter has no cure, you know."

It sounded so much like something Jen would say that Stephanie was annoyed and homesick all at the same time. "Ouch. I was being all supportive and plotting ways to assist you in your noble goals. Then you hit me with a low blow. Not cool."

Teresa held out both hands. "Hey, I have to call it like I see it, kid."

Stephanie squeezed her eyes shut. "You go for what you want, okay? I'm still trying to figure out what I want."

"Fair enough. That can be tricky, especially if he lives quite happily with spotty electricity and mostly cold water." Teresa stretched. "And now I go to make dinner. I'm craving pasta."

"You can never go wrong with pasta," Stephanie said. "I'll help."

"Of course you will. Daniel's certain to be very far away from the cooking. Thank goodness."

"He asked for space. I'm doing the best

I can." The answer sounded like a cop-out even to Stephanie's ears.

"Maybe you ought to take a long, hard look at how often you do the best you can for other people. Getting what you want sometimes means doing the best you can for yourself." Teresa sighed. "And now I'm done with the fortune-cookie pronouncements. I promise."

Stephanie smiled, but she was sure Teresa had hit on the biggest problem without any effort. After a lifetime of fitting in, playing it safe and keeping everyone around her happy, she'd have to rock the boat, upset people who loved her and take the biggest risk she could imagine...all for an uncertain outcome. Daniel was right. Whether or not things worked out the way she wanted, her life would never be the same.

If she went home as planned, went back to work and pretended she was content, at least she had something she could depend on.

But was that enough?

STEPHANIE HAD KEPT her promise to keep her distance, give him some space.

The problem was she'd done it entirely too well.

He missed her. He wanted to watch her sing and dance with the kids or wash dishes or even flop in the dirt if that was what she was doing. Instead, she was like a song he couldn't quite remember, always there in the background but he was never satisfied.

"What's the plan for today?" Teresa asked as she pushed back from the table, empty breakfast plate in hand. "Did you want to try to make it to Omas or wait for next week? We'll be short on supplies until you get back from Lima."

Daniel glanced over at Stephanie and quickly looked away. "Yeah. I could go back early, take the extra time to meet with the head of the university's medical school."

Stephanie would be gone that much sooner and he could start the grieving process early.

She'd probably welcome a hot shower and the chance to move around freely, no need to dodge the grumpy doctor.

"I could set up a dental clinic here in Alto. Some patients were left waiting when we closed up. A half day would do it. Teresa could do vision tests with the glasses we have on hand and Nicole could assist as needed." Weaver glanced at Nicole who nodded her agreement. "Then we can set out for Omas early next week, have a full day there."

Everyone was watching him closely.

Except Stephanie. She stared hard at the saltshaker.

If they had been on solid footing, she'd probably tell him to forget about cheating her out of a day. Loudly. And everyone would laugh along.

Instead, tense silence took over the kitchen.

He wasn't ready to say goobye.

"Why don't we take the day off? Go to San Pedro instead. It's a festival day so there should be plenty of excitement." Nicole clapped and even Stephanie straightened in her chair. He was on the right track. "Most of the town will be headed over there anyway. Not sure how many patients you'd see."

There'd be no reason to let Stephanie out of his sight. She'd need his protection, of course. "And I'll stop in to talk with the mayor and other officials to discuss these new science programs we'd like to get started in the schools, see if there's any interest." That was enough to ease the pinch of guilt at giving them all a day off.

"Some beautiful shots for color and atmosphere might be exactly what I need to make this fund-raising report pop." Stephanie eased around the table to head for the sink. "Good thinking, D."

He nodded like he'd been focused on his job, his calling, the reason he felt drawn to Peru.

Instead of thinking about her.

"Good ideas. I'm filled with them." He very obviously avoided Weaver's stare as he stood up. "Meet everyone out front in fifteen."

"And I'll buy you a drink," he heard Weaver say, the smile in his voice easy to pick up even as Daniel left the room.

Was he talking to Stephanie?

"What are we, chopped liver?" Teresa asked.

Of course he was talking to Stephanie.

Even though the laughter and chatter between the other members of his team was inviting, Daniel forced himself to walk away.

CHAPTER THIRTEEN

THE MOOD INSIDE the truck was more somber than she'd expected. In the kitchen, everyone had pitched in to clean up, and there'd been plenty of teasing about who would be buying the first round of drinks. She had no idea what to expect of a festival day in San Pedro but it sounded like one big party.

Were they talking Inca Kolas here or something that packed a punch? She'd hesitated to ask.

Now everyone had picked a window and was staring out it resolutely.

Except for her. She was in the middle again and stuck staring into the rearview mirror where all she could see was the small furrow between Daniel's eyebrows.

If he was the one dampening the mood, he was doing it silently.

To distract herself she leaned around Nicole to look out the window and watch the precarious edge of the road, not nearly as far from the tires as she'd like, as they slowly wound down to take another road, one they'd never traveled since she'd been in Alto.

"Wasn't this where the bus went off the edge?" Weaver asked and pointed, his arm waving in front of her face to show a washout on the side of the road. If it wasn't, it might be someday soon.

"Yes." Daniel glanced back in the rearview mirror for half a second and then back to the road.

"Sorry. I shouldn't have brought that up." Weaver patted her leg. "Don't worry. Daniel drives as well as he does everything else." His hand rested against her thigh as if they were old friends. Or more.

Until she brushed it off. He didn't say anything but the look he gave her combined hurt, disappointment and maybe a touch of wounded male ego.

Daniel muttered, "Change of subject, please."

Instead of immediately launching into something new, Weaver glanced at her, raised his eyebrows as though he wanted her to laugh and then shrugged. "Nice weather we're having."

For a second her eyes met Daniel's in the rearview mirror, and she could see just how tense he was.

She returned to staring out the window. But after a moment, she realized smoothing things over with Daniel would improve everyone's day. She owed it to her new friends to do the best she could. "So tell me about San Pedro. Is it larger than Alto?"

No one answered her at first. Eventually Daniel said, "Yes, the population's bigger and they have a doctor in town, so we haven't really explored the area. It's close enough for us, since we've got transportation, but most people don't have that. In Alto, the *colectivo* or bus runs on certain days and times so getting medical treatment here would be very difficult. If you miss the horn honking or it's too crowded to stand, you have no ride. And anyone who lives in Plata would first have to walk to Alto to catch the bus. But for a day like today? There would be a special run, a combi or truck or something, and it would be packed." He glanced at her in the mirror and looked back at the road ahead. "This festival will draw all kinds of visitors. People who've moved away will come home for a visit and they'll have vendors from Lima. You'll enjoy it."

Stephanie could tell he was smiling from the crinkles around his eyes. To reward him for the effort of stringing that many words together and using a friendly tone, she smiled back.

"We might see a soccer tournament, too," Nicole said. "Semiprofessional teams travel all over to play at these festivals." She turned to tease Stephanie. "Very cute players, too."

"Oh, good. Since I know nothing about soccer, at least I'll be able to enjoy the scenery."

Everyone but Daniel laughed and the tension in the truck eased enough for Stephanie to relax the firm grip she had on her knees.

Then they hit a solid line of traffic and she started to wonder how much weight the roads could handle. The winding trail led to a broad plain covered in green grass. Small buildings in the distance showed a town set up on a hill, but they'd found the action. Daniel managed to park the truck far enough away from the road for her comfort, and they all piled out of the vehicle.

Applause and shouts erupted from the crowd circling what had to be a soccer field. "Soccer. I knew it! It's going to be a good day," Nicole said with a sparkle in her eyes. Then she grabbed Daniel's arm and Teresa's hand and pulled them toward the action.

Weaver shoved his hands in his pockets and walked beside Stephanie.

"We're going to be pizza and beers kind of friends, aren't we?" he asked. "I'm not sure I've ever transitioned this fast before. We haven't even kissed yet."

Stephanie bumped her shoulder against his. "Do you really want to? I make an awesome friend."

He stopped in his tracks and then chuckled. "Well, way to kill a man's ego. Yeah, I did or I wouldn't have asked for your number. Just my luck to find the prettiest girl in the Andes who's in love with another man. And that's before she even steps off the plane."

"If it helps, I know how you feel, Weaver," Stephanie said and patted him on the back. "We're both going to recover."

There was no point in denying what he'd said. She was in love with Daniel. No other man stirred up the butterflies in her stomach.

Not a single date had made her feel as comfortable or as strong or as beautiful as Daniel had by telling her she was the kind of woman who could change a life.

"Are you sure you'll recover?" Weaver asked.

Instead of pretending she didn't know what he was talking about, she shrugged. "I'll have my whole life to figure that out, I guess."

"Well, we're still going for pizza. Maybe you'll change your mind. A dentist in the hand being worth at least one hero far, far away and all that." Weaver wrapped an arm around her shoulder. Stephanie stumbled, but he managed to pull her closer to his side to steady her.

"She's made it clear that you should keep your hands off, Weaver." Daniel's voice was cold. The crowd disappeared and all that was left was the three of them, her and two angry men.

"He was saving me from a fall, Daniel. Like any good friend would do." She smiled over her shoulder at Weaver, stepped away from him and swept around Daniel in what she hoped was a regal manner. "Someone come explain soccer to me."

"I don't know much, but I can make up the rules. That'll be pretty entertaining," Weaver said. "Come on, Daniel. You can keep me on my toes."

Daniel didn't immediately follow, but she waited for him to make up his mind. Eventually the tension in his shoulders eased. "You go ahead. I've got some business to attend to first."

Stephanie led the way to Nicole and Teresa, who had their heads together, whispering. Instead of jumping to the conclusion that they were talking about her and the never-before-seen-phenomenon of two handsome men tense-talking over her, she asked, "Which team has the cuter players? I assume that's who we're rooting for."

Teresa straightened immediately, a light blush on her cheekbones. "Uh, we haven't decided. What do you think?"

So they had been talking about her. Stephanie cleared her throat and waited.

"Sorry." Teresa grabbed Stephanie's hands. "We were gossiping. I'm really sorry. It won't happen again." She crossed her heart and nodded enthusiastically.

The three of them turned to watch the action on the field for a minute.

"But Daniel... Don't you think his jealousy was a sign of something? I mean, those guys are pretty good friends," Nicole asked as she leaned around Teresa.

Stephanie glanced from Teresa to Nicole and figured there were no real secrets between them.

"Doesn't matter. We're still separated by a whole lot of distance."

Even on his day off—the last she'd be spending in the mountains with him and her new friends—he'd put his mission first.

She surveyed the crowd to track him down and saw his head above a small group of older men, most of whom were nodding enthusiastically.

The huge grin he wore as he waved good-bye to them and started in her direction was unexpected.

The way her heart sped up when he came over and the dumb urge to stare at her feet was less shocking.

"Success. I'm going to bring the next crew to the elementary school and then the high school to do a program for the students." He held up his hand for a high five.

She couldn't leave him hanging. "All right. That's great news! Now all we have to do is set up a program."

"I have faith you'll get us exactly what we need to start the program." He wrapped an arm over her shoulder and pulled her closer. "Thank you for blackmailing me into making this trip. Could be the best thing that ever happened to HealthyAmericas."

And just like that, she was tumbling again.

That was the thing about heroes. When they were shining, their flaws didn't matter anymore. For two more days she'd be head over heels. There was no real hope for any different outcome.

Then when she made it home she'd get real.

DANIEL STOOD WITH one arm braced against the wrought iron fence surrounding the small green area in the middle of San Pedro, satisfied with his day. Teresa, Nicole and Stephanie were haggling with a vendor over a woven tapestry. He could see a lot of frowning as the three of them weeded through words that Teresa knew and discarded the ones that didn't support their cause.

He should help, but it was nice to see Stephanie standing tall and slowly but surely winning over the little old man who stared at her long blond hair in amazement.

When she suddenly waved off his latest offer as if she was done bargaining and handed the man nuevo soles in exchange for the wall hanging, he could tell that she'd overpaid—even from this distance. The man slowly wrapped up her tapestry, presented it to her with a flourish and bent to press a kiss to the back of her hand. Instead of jerking her hand back, probably the first impulse of most women, she cheerfully said, *"Gracias!"* She waved over her shoulder and made a straight line for Daniel.

"Any advice to keep a small Peruvian man from trying to hide away in my suitcase," Stephanie asked.

He bent down to murmur in her ear, "How much money did you give him?"

"Way too much obviously." But the vendor was now flirting with another group of women. "And he's already moved on."

"Bullfight!" Weaver called out, hurrying toward them. "Come on. We can't miss this!" He pointed in the direction most people were slowly flowing. "I'll grab us some seats." He, Teresa and Nicole plunged into the crowd.

"What do you think? Are you up for some more adventure?" Daniel asked.

"For a bullfight?" Stephanie grimaced. "Not my thing. One way or the other, there's a loser and I'm not sure who to vote for." She shrugged. "But I'm probably pro-bull. He never said, 'Hey, I'd like to try to murder someone today.' Life worked out that way, you know?"

Daniel frowned as he considered that. It had the unique flavor of Stephanie logic, but he thought he followed. "If it was a mass puppy-petting, you'd be the first in line."

She nodded. "Exactly. Or even if it was a bull-petting, although I imagine they'd have more trouble finding volunteers for that."

"So, no bullfights." Daniel patted the spot next to him. "We'll sit here instead."

Stephanie sighed as she leaned against the fence. "I'd tell you to go and leave me here, but we both know how well that would work."

Daniel grunted but shook his head in amusement.

"Ever since our argument and the emergency, I've been…confused. I want to apologize for distracting you, but I need to make you understand who I am now."

Daniel opened his mouth and then closed it. The brush of his arm against hers eased some of her jitters.

"I shouted at you," he said. "But I was mad at myself."

Stephanie raised her eyebrows. "We're both pretty good at apologizing without admitting fault. Something else we have in common."

She was right. They had a lot in common.

Stephanie tilted her head back to study the darkening sky. "Harder to see the stars here with all this excess electricity."

San Pedro had six streetlights surrounding the square and the line of vendors had strung up lights from one end of the road to the other in order to show off their wares. "I imagine the lights of Holly Heights will take some getting used to again."

"You'd be surprised how easy it is to adjust to comfort," Daniel said. "I learned that quickly enough on my first return to Lima."

They were quiet as cheers erupted from outside the town. Daniel didn't want to speculate what might be causing the celebration.

"Think you'll ever move home?" Stephanie asked without turning toward him. "Or even come for a visit. Your sister misses you."

Daniel thought about explaining that he'd never seriously considered coming home until she'd landed in his hotel lobby. "Some days it's all I can think about. Lately my reasons for staying are less satisfying."

Neither one of them spoke for a long time.

"I wish I had more time here. I understand a little of why you stay, what drives you to ignore the inconveniences and missing home. Even on your day off, you work first, then play. So dedicated."

"Here's the thing." He watched her studying the night sky as though she was preparing to take a test. Or more likely, avoiding him as best she could. "Coming back with my tail between my legs isn't me, but lately I've been wondering if it's duty or fear that makes it hard to think of going home."

"Fear of your mistakes? Is that it?"

"Sort of, but it's more about losing the respect I had." How dumb. "Blowing that… It's hard to recover from. I have respect here. It's safe here."

Stephanie snorted. "Good grief, Daniel. I thought you were this brave hero and you're as scared as the rest of us. What a realization for you, to find out you're plain human after all."

"You aren't scared, are you? The whole

world tells you to stay in Holly Heights and you do what you want anyway. How did you get so brave?" Daniel touched her shoulder. He wanted to see her face.

"I decided there was something I wanted more than safety, Daniel." She turned to look at him and shrugged. "Not that I understood until this second here with you. I was afraid to get on the plane. I was petrified to try bluffing my way into your truck, mainly because I was so scared you were going to treat me differently than you always have. Before you left I thought I knew you well enough to call it love, but after this trip I know you better than I ever have." She shook her head sadly. "And I like you even more, even though you wish I'd never come."

Before he could argue, she added, "And even more important, I know myself better than I ever have. I'm not going to be content with the things people tell me I should be content with. I've already tried it that way and failed.

"Caring about what other people think instead of what I know to be true is a failure."

She watched him carefully, and he knew why a second later, when he realized she was talking about him, too.

He'd been playing it safe in Alto. He made the rules here, and if something made him uncomfortable, like the emotions an old friend stirred up, he backed away as quickly as he could.

"You've made such an impact here and I hope you'll continue to contribute…from wherever this new plan takes you. I need your help to make this work," he said.

"Not just my money?" she asked with a grin.

"Well, I'm not gonna say your money isn't truly lovely, but the reports you've been building…they blow anything I could have drafted out of the water."

Stephanie raised her eyebrows and said, "So my ignoring your rules can be forgiven?"

"Forgiven, yes, but never forgotten." His lips twitched as she sniffed in response. "Seriously, you're welcome on my team in my town at any time, Steph."

"Really? That's huge." She patted his arm.

"Want to go ahead and say you were wrong, too?"

"Nope."

Under better circumstances they would've both laughed. Now he was happy the tension had eased a bit.

"Since you've conquered Alto, I expect to hear stories of you globe-trotting and spreading philanthropy everywhere you go." Daniel rubbed at his chest to chase away the ache that bloomed at the thought of missing whatever she did next.

"Well, you don't want me to stay here, with you. You've made that clear." She stared into his eyes, and he was almost certain she wanted him to disagree. Was she waiting for him to ask her to stay?

He was saved from answering when the crowd of bullfight spectators began trickling back into the center of town.

"That was fast." Daniel pulled Stephanie closer as the music started up and so did the dancing.

Weaver, Nicole and Teresa joined them. "The bull...it escaped the ring!" Weaver's announcement stopped Daniel in his tracks.

"What now?" He scanned the crowd. No one seemed the least concerned. "But they caught him, penned him up somewhere?"

"Nope. I imagine he's halfway to Lima by now. That sucker could move when he got the chance," Weaver said.

All three women took a step closer to Daniel. "You don't think a bull on the loose is something to worry about, do you?" Nicole asked as she glanced over her shoulder. When she turned back to him, ready to hear his easy assurance, Daniel realized she was going to believe whatever he had to say.

"Sure, no worries, Nicole." He watched all three women nod, but no one seemed to relax.

"To be safe, let's head back to Alto. Weaver, you ready?" Daniel stood slowly and had to repeat himself over the music. Before Weaver could answer, the crowd scattered as a man who'd had a few too many drinks rolled down the hill into the town square. "And we can get an early start tomorrow."

He had to shout the last sentence so he didn't even wait for agreement but started working his way through the crowd. Stephanie's sharp fingernails on his waist reassured him that he wouldn't lose her. One glance back showed Teresa and Nicole close behind Stephanie with Weaver bringing up the rear.

Before they made it to the truck, he could see a large group gathered around it. A quick conversation made it clear that all the people were headed back to Alto and they'd very much like a ride. Instead of arguing, he motioned at the bed of the truck and watched the people pile in. "Everybody in."

When his crew was loaded inside, one small woman remained. If he had to guess, he'd say she was the grandmother who ran the store in Alto. Climbing up into the bed of the truck would be impossible for her. He glanced in the rearview mirror, about to ask Weaver to take one for the team, when Stephanie shoved open the front passenger side door. "Climb in, Tamaya." She motioned for the woman to climb in and managed to stifle a grunt as the woman clambered up to drop beside her.

His lips were twitching when Stephanie glanced his way.

"Coca-Cola." The little woman pointed at her chest and smiled broadly at Stephanie.

He wondered if that was an offer to buy her a Coke on her next visit.

Then he realized Stephanie wouldn't be making any more visits to the store in Alto, and he was sad all over again.

The drive up to Alto was silent.

And very, very dark.

At one point, Stephanie gasped in alarm and he reached over to take her hand in his. He wished he'd done the same the first time they'd traveled in the dark. Or every time he'd had a chance. He'd known from the beginning that he'd miss her when she went, so he'd tried to protect himself and her.

What he should have been doing was building memories.

Maybe that had always been his problem.

But what was he going to do about it?

When the truck rolled to a stop in front of the municipal building, the people in the bed scattered. Weaver carefully helped Tamaya down from the front seat and escorted Teresa and Nicole over the bumpy ground up to the municipal building.

"You okay? We made it. You can open your eyes." He watched Stephanie carefully stretch.

"Not sure I remember what it's like to have blood flow to my right foot. Every single minute around this place is unexpected, isn't it?"

"I gotta say, since you came here that's been true." Unexpected and exciting.

"Admit it. You're going to miss me when I'm gone." She slid out of the truck and slammed the door. "No need to pretend otherwise."

He walked around the truck and grabbed her hand before she could turn away.

"I am. I will. Never doubt that, Stephanie." He shrugged. "If this trip was about showing me a different side of you, I've seen it. You're strong. Brave. Beautiful. If things were different... I don't know, but I sort of wish they were."

She snorted. "This trip... It did start as a way to prove that you can't hurt me. Or not for long, anyway. But what I didn't understand at the beginning—and what you don't seem to get right now—is that this trip should have been about us not me."

"There shouldn't be an us. You deserve a generous man, not one who refuses to change the way he thinks." And she'd find him. He had all the faith in the world that she would charge after what she wanted.

"You think that guy exists, do you?" She tilted her head. "Here's the thing. We're all selfish. But when we love someone, we want them to be happy. We do things to ensure that happiness. And we change because of the people we love."

"Love" hung there in the space between them until Daniel cleared his throat awkwardly.

"And on that note, I believe I'll wish you a good-night. We aren't going to solve anything here. Why do I waste my breath?"

Before Daniel could hurry forward to catch her arm, ask her to stand still while he found the right words to explain, Stephanie marched up the dark hill to the municipal building. He wanted to chase after her, but he had no idea what to say.

Instead he propped his hands on his hips and watched her struggle up the rocky hill.

When she fell, he was too far away to catch her, but he could hear the pained gasp as she hit the ground and skidded toward him.

His heart racing, Daniel ran to her side, coming to rest painfully on his knees in the rocky dirt.

"What happened? Are you hurt?" He hesitated before running his hands over her ankles and calves to check for broken bones.

"Only my pride." Stephanie cursed under her breath. "And my wrist. Possibly all of the skin on both hands and my left knee."

Daniel bent his head forward to try to slow his pulse. She didn't need panic. She needed a doctor.

"Here. I'll carry you inside." Daniel shifted forward to ease his hands under her legs, but her hard grip stopped him.

"Don't even." She huffed out an angry breath. "That's all we need. A doctor who breaks his neck or his back while trying to rescue the damsel. I'll walk."

Even if he'd much rather have cradled her

close for a long second to reassure himself that she'd escaped real injury this time, Daniel knew very well that she needed control.

"If you're sure. You're zero for one on this hill tonight, remember. Maybe walking isn't in the cards for you." Daniel stood and brushed the rocks off his jeans, then reached under her arms to lift her so that she could stand.

The fact that she leaned against him to get her balance confirmed how shaken up Stephanie was. She tried a weak elbow to his abdomen to make him back off, but he wrapped his arm around her shoulder and carried as much of her weight as she'd let him up the steep hill.

Inside the well-lit municipal building, Stephanie's face was pale. The scrapes on her hands were gritty and red. And the way she held her left arm carefully against her chest worried him.

"What happened?" Teresa asked as she stuck her head out of the kitchen.

"I fell. Like an idiot. Almost made it through the entire trip without hurting myself, and I ruined my record in the front yard." Stephanie groaned as she sat in one of the folding chairs at the card table. "Stupid."

An X-ray machine. That was what he needed. And if she needed surgery to set a broken bone, she was in for a long night and day.

"Let me see." Daniel gently pried her arm away from her chest and stretched it carefully on the table.

"I think I felt something pop." Stephanie bit her lip and sniffled, but the tears in her eyes didn't spill over.

"Grab the ice pack," Daniel said over his shoulder to Teresa. He needed a minute. Unless he could get himself under control, he was going to be crying harder than his patient.

He couldn't look at her face, so he carefully studied her wrist and arm, probing gently to make sure nothing was broken. "Move your fingers."

He watched them shift on the table.

"Do you think it's a sprain?" Stephanie had to clear her throat after her voice cracked. "Of course it is. It's just a sprain."

Teresa reached around him to set the gel

ice pack carefully over Stephanie's wrist. Then she set down a rolled bandage and stepped back to watch with her arms crossed over her chest.

Business. Keep this business, Daniel. Everyone's watching to see how you handle this.

"Here's what we're going to do." He picked up the bandage. "Anti-inflammatories tonight. We'll compress it to keep it stable. Ice to help with swelling. We've got another pack, right?" He glanced at Teresa to see her sympathetic face. When she nodded, he did, too. "If you can get any sleep tonight, try to keep the wrist above your heart, just to help with swelling. Switch out the ice pack when this one melts."

He stood. "Then tomorrow we'll visit the hospital in Lima, get an X-ray and a cast if you need it." He shook his head. "That's the best we can do here."

Stephanie bit her lip and then tried a brave smile. The tears brightening her eyes made it hard to return that smile.

"I'm sorry, Daniel. What a klutz."

"Those look like some serious scrapes,"

Teresa said while he tried to figure out how to tell Stephanie she had nothing to apologize for. Accidents happened, but this was the reason she couldn't stay. He wouldn't be able to stand it if something more serious happened to her.

He opened his mouth to try to say something, but Teresa set a hand on his shoulder. "Why don't I work on cleaning up the scrapes? If we need you, I'll call you."

Stephanie didn't look up from her careful study of the ice pack. "Wrap the wrist first," he said.

"You got it." Teresa tilted her chin down. "Go."

He nodded and raced up the stairs two at a time. To avoid Weaver, he ducked into the tiny bathroom in the men's dorm and braced both hands on the sink.

Panicking like this was unacceptable. If Stephanie had been seriously hurt, his emotional attachment might have interfered with his training.

But there was no way to eliminate the emotional attachment. Not now. She had to go back to Texas. He was fooling himself to believe he would ever be able to keep her safe. She was smart and strong, but in Holly Heights the care she'd need was closer than a day's drive down treacherous roads.

He did love her.

Now there was no question.

That meant wanting her safety and happiness more than his own.

Stephanie belonged in Texas.

STEPHANIE TRIED NOT to whimper as Teresa wrapped the bandage around her wrist. Once it was fastened, she eased back against the chair and took her first deep breath. "That feels better."

Teresa nodded and slid the ice pack back over her wrist. "Let's see those knees."

For half a second Stephanie thought about protesting for modesty's sake. This was no doctor's office, but she was too tired and discouraged to waste her energy on dumb protests.

Teresa helped her with the jeans and then sucked in a breath at the angry scrapes over both knees. "You don't mess around, do you?"

Don't cry. Don't be the weak girl who cries over scrapes and bruises.

But it was useless. All this insistence that she was strong and independent and she was brought low by tripping on her own feet.

The first tear streaked down her cheek, but Stephanie angrily brushed it away. Daniel couldn't even look at her. He was probably shoring up his defenses at the moment, thanks to this proof that he'd been right all along.

She was too delicate for Peru.

"This might sting," Teresa said as she cleaned the scrapes.

They were both quiet until Teresa stepped back. "I think you're going to live, patient."

"Thanks, doc." Stephanie sniffed and added, "I believe you're right. Toss me an anti-inflammatory and maybe I'll be convinced this was all a bad dream in the morning."

The rattle of pills was loud in the empty room. Teresa disappeared and returned with a bottle of water. "Take this. Drink the whole thing."

Water, the cure-all on the mountain.

Stephanie followed orders and tried to come up with a way to breeze out of the room, but Teresa sat down next to her and propped her chin on her hand to wait patiently.

"I don't want to talk about it. I'm going home tomorrow. Everything will return to normal for all of us." Stephanie chanced a look up to see whether Teresa was going to accept that.

Teresa just pursed her lips.

Stephanie's shoulders slumped. "I think I'm most upset that I ruined my grand exit."

Teresa's chuckle made her laugh, too.

"Now he knows he was right. I can't make it here. If I were here, he'd have to watch over me the whole time. I've just proven every one of his objections."

Teresa shrugged. "Not really. There's still time. Didn't some wise person say it's not how you fall down in the dark but how you recover in the daylight that proves who you are?"

Stephanie frowned. "I'm pretty sure that's not how it goes."

"Maybe I just made up a new thing, then."

Teresa squeezed her shoulder. "I'm very wise."

"Help me upstairs?" Stephanie was too discouraged to joke anymore. She wanted rest. She wanted to magically be transported to Holly Heights without having to meet Daniel's concerned, unhappy stare.

For the first time since she'd fallen in love with Alto and with Daniel all over again, she wished she'd never thrown the dart in the first place.

CHAPTER FOURTEEN

SAYING GOODBYE TO Teresa had been difficult, but ignoring the way Daniel walked behind her, both hands ready to catch her, was even worse. At least it took her mind off her throbbing wrist for a bit.

A long night of cursing her misstep and replaying Daniel's reaction meant her head ached worse than her wrist anyway. Business as usual. That was the only way to make it through the drive. The mix of pain, homesickness, sadness at waving goodbye to new friends, and the prospect of seeing Daniel for the last time, all added up to a combustible tangle of emotions. She had to focus on work.

Instead of holding on to any stable surface, Stephanie ignored the view and went through the long list of things that still needed to be finalized when she made it back to Texas. It was no formal agenda, but having the to-do list made it simpler to avoid talking about feelings and the future.

She had a hunch Daniel might put her out on the nonexistent side of the road if she accidentally brushed up against emotions.

"We don't have to do this now," Daniel said, his grim tone matching his face.

Everything he said was perfectly businesslike and detached. He gripped the steering wheel so tightly she was afraid one big bump and he'd rip it completely off.

Taking it so seriously might be a good thing.

And if she hadn't already ridden with him when he was so carelessly confident, she might even buy it.

"We don't have much time. And neither one of us wants to talk about anything else, that's for sure." Stephanie rolled her eyes and flipped the page of her notes. As long as she held her hand close to her heart, her wrist barely hurt. That made writing with the other hand as they bounced along nearly impossible, but she'd worry about deciphering her scribbles later. The distraction would be welcome.

"All right, when I make the final changes to this, adding in the statistics on childhood mortality and the falling rates of childhood illness, I'll email it to you. Would you like me to send it to anyone else?" She clicked her pen, ready to take down notes like a perfect, emotionless secretary. She also stopped herself from grunting when the truck lurched over a gnarly pothole.

"Yes, please copy Dr. Claudia Wright." He rattled off an email address before the truck slid to a stop at the busy paved highway. Lima and the hotel lobby were looming in her near future. "She's planning a large event in two weeks and I owe her this, so if you can send it as soon as you get home, that would be a big help."

No orders. A request. Interesting.

Also, now she had the founder's email. She could advocate on Teresa's behalf.

And her own if she could figure out what she wanted.

"Should I pass along any fussy words to your sister? Make sure she knows you

don't appreciate her sending along spies?"
Rebecca was going to be disappointed that
she didn't have news of an imminent arrival,
but she wouldn't be surprised.

"No." The muscle in his jaw flexed as he
made the right turn and accelerated to match
the rest of traffic whizzing by.

"I know you don't want to go to the hospital here in Lima." The steering wheel
squeaked as his hands twisted. "And I understand trusting the care in Holly Heights,
but I would rather make sure you're okay
before you get on a plane. I won't leave your
side."

They'd already had this very short argument once. Her answer hadn't changed.

"No. I want to go home." She did. She
wanted to lick her wounds in her safe spot.
Rebecca would make her a cookie and the
disappointment at the way the whole trip
ended would be easier to bear. "And it's really not bothering me." Much. A little. And
by the time she made it to Holly Heights she
would no doubt curse her decision, but she
was going to stick to it.

Daniel's look made it clear he wasn't buying her story.

Frustrated and a little annoyed that he couldn't help her make this easier, she turned to study the ocean waves crashing on the shore. Here the sunshine was gone and gray skies cast a film over the beautiful scenery. A light mist covered the windshield, so Daniel turned the wipers on.

"At least the weather fits the mood," Stephanie said.

He grunted.

"Or maybe that's just me. You could be dancing on the inside at the chance to get back to your routine." She shoved her ragged journal, the one that had been in such pristine condition the last time she was in Lima, inside her dusty backpack. "While I am dancing on the inside at the promise of a hot shower, clean clothes and a trip to the airport." Flying at night would not have been her choice, mainly because it would put her arrival time in Houston so early, but at least she'd make it back to Holly Heights at a reasonable time, even after driving home.

Maybe this time, she'd be able to sleep. Better pain medication would help.

"I'm not dancing at all. I'll miss you. And I'm pretty sure what used to be comfortable won't fit me anymore. I blame you for that." His grip tightened on the steering wheel.

She whistled. "Tell me how you really feel."

"Okay." He opened his mouth and hesitated, then blurted, "I don't want you to leave. Let's go to the hospital. Stay here, recuperate. Give me time to figure things out. When I bring Weaver, Nicole and Teresa back, we can do some sightseeing. Maybe get to know each other better."

She didn't know what to say.

"That's how I really feel," he muttered.

At first, the all-out joy that flooded through her made it hard to catch her breath. He wanted her to stay. That was huge, right?

Then she studied his grim face and realized it was huge but nothing was settled. Nothing would be settled until they both figured out what they wanted.

"Then, after we see everything Lima has to offer, what do we do?" She squeezed her eyes shut to prepare herself. "And why couldn't I just stay with you in Alto? If you want time together, doesn't that make more sense?"

"I have no idea." His sigh leaked out slowly, perfectly matching the way her excitement faded. "I do want more time with you." He glanced at her wrapped wrist and Stephanie knew neither one of them had changed their minds. He didn't think she was safe in Alto. She didn't want to be his little sister or some kind of burden.

And she'd been waiting long enough. For the longest time she'd waited for him to notice her as something other than a pesky sidekick. Then she'd waited for her life to become what she wanted it to be.

Now she could spend two weeks waiting for him to come back.

Or she could get on with living the life she wanted.

Before she'd completely made up her mind, he pulled into the driveway of the small business-class hotel and parked. They were both quiet as he turned off the engine.

"You know what it's like to put off a project because it feels too big or it'll take too much time or it's something small that you hate, and you make a list of all the other chores that have to be done right this minute?" She turned to face him.

His blank expression was enough of an answer.

"Of course not. You don't even know what the word procrastination means, do you?" Stephanie reached over to take his hand. "But that's what this would be. Putting off the inevitable because it feels big. But it's really not. You've told me more than once there's no other way this works."

He tangled his fingers through hers. "What if I'm wrong? This one time."

The temptation was so dangerous. She could explore the city, take a tour to Machu Picchu, update her blog and generally behave like the world expected a lottery winner to behave. And at the end, Daniel would join her and they could see if they had a future together.

On the other hand, plans had been hazily forming in her brain.

Plans that had to do with her future.

If she stayed in Lima, she'd be acting like the old Stephanie—the woman who was prepared to wait for what she wanted to magically find her instead of going after it.

"Tell you what. Next time you're in Texas, call me. We'll get dressed up and hit the town. No pizza and beer. No Rebecca and Jen. Just you and me." She squeezed his hand. "Maybe we'll have everything figured out by then."

Keeping her breathing even and her smile steady took every bit of the strength she had.

"Why is it so important to do that in Texas?" He frowned. "I thought this offer would make you happy."

"That's why you growled it out as if you were giving me bad news." She rolled her eyes. "You don't know what you want. It's okay. I'm in the same boat. I'm saying we need to figure that out before we take a crazy risk on falling more in love so far from home. I'm saying you were right, Dr. Lincoln. You like that."

His lips tightened as he shook his head slowly. "I can't argue with you. That's disappointing."

She squeezed her right hand together to hide the jitters. Unless she got out of this truck quickly, her emotions were going to break through her control.

She might even change her mind about staying.

"Listen, for two weeks you're committed. Go do your job. Meet with the medical school director. Finalize plans in the villages for the science programs. Cure the sick. It's not like you'll have a lot of spare time. Then come back to Lima and decide what you want. If you're up for a trip to Texas, we'll both know things between us have gone beyond pesky sidekick and annoyed older brother.

"Meanwhile, I'm headed for a shower and as much sightseeing as I can cram in before my flight. You are not to worry about me. I'll send you an email with the finalized reports tomorrow." If she didn't get out of this truck immediately, she would either burst into tears or…give in. Sit back. Wait.

She put one hand on the door, but he pulled her over the console in a hard hug. Then he said, "Go. Now. Before I try to change your mind. Head for Texas, but whatever you do, stop waiting. You deserve everything you want. This time, follow the rules. Go."

"Always so noble." She shook her head. "I think we might have our answer. Duty will always come first. That's what makes you who you are. I'll make sure Dr. Wright gets the checks you've earned. Thanks for showing me your world." Before he could say anything else, Stephanie waved her bandaged hand and slid out of the truck.

DANIEL WATCHED STEPHANIE disappear inside the hotel and fought the urge to follow her. He could check with Paulo, make sure all her things were accounted for. Then he could ask for the room he always used to be given to her. He'd determined the hot water to be most reliable on the lower floors, something she wouldn't know. Someone should help her with all her luggage here at the hotel and at the airport. And the idea of her sightseeing alone in a city the size of Lima made his stomach hurt.

She was smart, but Holly Heights was a

small place. The traffic alone in Lima took a lot of getting used to.

But she didn't need his protection. She'd proven it more than once.

Right now, he had a job. He pulled his cell phone out of the console and checked for a signal. The thing was useless in Alto, but here the connection was strong. First he dialed his contact at the health ministry and asked for an introduction to the medical director. While he waited for his contact to return the call with plans for a dinner meeting, he drove over to the medical supplies warehouse to pick up the order he'd placed the last time he was in Lima.

Stephanie was right. He had an important job to do. And if he wanted to do anything else, something that made him happy instead of filling the need to make a difference, he was going to have to build in some time.

After a long afternoon of straightening out the supply order, something he had to do every single time, and dinner at the loudest American-style restaurant in town with his health ministry contact and the medical school director, Daniel was beat. He trudged through the hotel lobby.

At this hour Stephanie would already be at the airport.

If she'd gone through with it.

He leaned against the lobby desk. Paulo was off duty, but the night guy recognized him. "*Hola*, Dr. Lincoln. How may I help?"

"I wanted to check on a traveler. Has Stephanie Yates already checked out?"

Daniel rubbed his forehead as he listened to the click-clack of keyboard keys. "Yes, sir. She left almost two hours ago to return home." The man smiled. "A very pretty lady, as I recall."

Daniel grunted in response. "Thanks. I'll check in, too."

The man slid a key across the desk. "You're already checked in. Let me get your bags."

CHAPTER FIFTEEN

FLYING AT NIGHT had one big advantage. At this hour fewer people were alert enough to see the evidence of her tears.

Crying about coming home was ridiculous. She loved Holly Heights, her family. And once she made it through baggage claim, her two best friends in the world would be waiting. There was too much to anticipate and so much work to be done that she had no reason for sadness.

But every photo she'd flipped through had reminded her who she was leaving.

Reading between the lines in her journal, she could see how small events had changed the way she saw the world and herself.

And the annoyed stick figure, complete with eye roll, she'd doodled on the edge of the reports she'd discussed with Daniel made her chuckle.

He wasn't perfect.

Neither was she.

But together they worked.

The flight was uneventful. She waited patiently for the plane to clear before making her way slowly down the aisle and through the airport to get her suitcases. Nothing felt the same, but everything was so familiar she could do it on autopilot.

An anxious businessman jostled her as he reached over to grab his suitcase and she was reminded she was now in Texas. She'd better get with the program. Her bags were zooming toward her so she lugged them off with her good hand and took a deep breath.

She had one more important job to do before she went home, showered for six hours and then slept for twelve.

She was about to see Daniel's sister. She had to fake not being in love better than she'd ever faked it before.

After carefully arranging the bags with all the clothes she hadn't needed, Stephanie moved slowly through the airport until she saw Rebecca and Jen waving outside the window. Then the tears started and she couldn't stop them.

"Hey, we're so happy you're home!" Jen hugged her hard and took one precarious stack of luggage. "What happened here?"

She pointed at the bandage on Stephanie's wrist.

"You know me. I tripped and landed on my hand and my dignity. Luckily, there was a doctor nearby."

Jen paused to study her face as the crowd flowed around them. Then she brushed Stephanie's hand away from the luggage cart. "Rebecca's got the car running, so we don't get towed away. Come on."

Grateful for Jen's matter-of-fact tone, Stephanie hustled to follow her and hugged Rebecca as Jen tossed all the bags in the car. "Let's get out of here. I hate this place," Rebecca muttered with a dark glare at the airport terminal.

No one said much as Rebecca carefully navigated the Houston traffic. Once they were outside the city, Stephanie said, "I expected you guys to roll up in a luxury sedan." She patted the worn upholstery of

Rebecca's passenger seat. "No time for car shopping yet?" she asked.

"Not yet. This one's no good at helping me pick something like that," Jen said as she motioned at Rebecca. "I was waiting on you."

"Great. Shopping with an unlimited budget. That'll be a new experience."

Her answer must have been disappointing because Rebecca glanced over. "We've got plenty of time to shop until we drop. Tell us about Peru. And Daniel. And your injury."

"The blog is awesome, Steph," Jen said from the backseat. "Would you have ever imagined doing the things you did?"

Grateful to have a chance to decompress and talk about the amazing, scary, life-changing experience, Stephanie launched into a blow-by-blow retelling of every single day.

Rebecca made sympathetic noises when she got to her tumble down the hill. Jen said, "Could have happened to anyone, Steph."

She thought about explaining how Daniel could barely look at her as he tried to treat her and how that made her feel as though maybe he'd been right all along, but that would lead to real talk about her feelings.

Her emotions were still too unsettled for that.

So she described Alto and the kids and the roads and the weather. And she had the best friends in the world, because neither of them yawned, stared off into space while composing a grocery list or interrupted to catch her up on the latest Holly Heights news. Instead they asked questions and laughed in all the right spots, and when she started to cry, even Jen tried to comfort her.

"Is this about…just, so much emotion? Or is this about something else?" Rebecca asked as she took the exit for Holly Heights. "You haven't said much about Daniel. Teresa sounds great and this Weaver guy has possibilities, but…"

Stephanie stared out the window and watched the shops on Holly Heights's main street flow by as she tried to figure out how to answer that. Neither of her friends pushed, but they both insisted on following her into to her spotless apartment and dropping her dusty luggage on the living room floor.

Then all three of them collapsed while they waited for Stephanie to figure out the answer.

It was impossible to pretend with Rebecca and Jen. "I love him." She sighed and closed her eyes. "This guy, he's real. And I love him. And that's all there is to that."

The long heavy silence that followed made her open her eyes to see both Rebecca and Jen watching her tensely.

"Well, what are you going to do about it?" Jen finally asked loudly, as if the waiting was too much.

Rebecca shook her head. "If she knew that she wouldn't look so miserable."

Jen opened her mouth to argue, probably with sound advice on storming Daniel's castle or something. Rebecca interrupted. "No luck in getting him to consider coming home, then?"

"If you could see him in action, you'd understand there's no better place for him. He's different in Alto. He's open and cares for his patients with such concern." Stephanie rubbed her dry, tired eyes.

Jen raised an eyebrow. "I have a hard time imagining him covered in dirt."

"I have pictures. The Daniel you think you know, he's different. Better. More." Stephanie shook her head. "And there's no way I could be the reason he'd give that up."

"I know what you mean," Rebecca said softly. "That's the real trouble with loving him. More should be his middle name."

They all smiled because it was true.

"Then what do we do? How do we fix this?" Jen asked. It was clear she was ready to fight the odds. Jen might seem to be reserved, the cool customer, but for her friends she'd charge into battle at the first war cry.

"There's one way." Rebecca wiped at a tear. "Stephanie's going back to Peru."

"No way!" Jen jerked up and paused on the edge of her seat. "That's impossible."

It was inevitable. And the sooner she surrendered to that, the easier the whole process would be. This was the problem Stephanie had been wrestling with since her first day in Alto. She was tired of fighting. Rebecca was right.

Since Jen's was the reaction she'd been expecting, Stephanie didn't argue. Convincing Jen and Rebecca would be the easiest part of her new plan, even if it was already off to a rocky start. The next wave—her family and all the committees that depended on her—would be harder, but if she could count on Jen and Rebecca, she could manage it.

"Not impossible. Difficult." Rebecca sighed. "But worth it."

Stephanie met Rebecca's stare. "With your help it won't even be that difficult."

"All this for a man? That's so silly. He will come back." Jen stood to pace while she cracked her knuckles, an old, bad habit. "Give me a shot. I'll get him back here." Her tone said he might find himself tied up with a thick rope, but it was hard to ignore her determination. "We belong together. And we belong here in Holly Heights. It's home."

Rebecca didn't answer, but she pulled out her phone and started to read some of Stephanie's last blog. "'Saying goodbye is unacceptable, so I'll say until I see you again.' This shouldn't be so surprising, Jen. If you didn't see it, it's because you didn't want to."

"Well, of course I didn't want to. If she

goes to Peru, you'll never see her because you can't get on an airplane without restraints, and I'll have to go all by myself." Jen flopped back down. "That's a lot of pressure, you guys."

Stephanie and Rebecca traded a look before they laughed.

When Jen joined them, Stephanie had a feeling the only piece of the plan she'd truly been worried about was going to fall into place.

"If I go, I'll come back." Stephanie knew there was no way she could say goodbye to home and Holly Heights even if Jen and Rebecca traveled with her. "But I have a plan. It's a big one. And I'm going to need some checks, possibly some moral support and a shopping trip. We're going to a fund-raiser where I will sell myself so hard that Healthy-Americas will have no choice but to make a job for me."

She shrugged. "I believe this is what we call a long shot."

Jen dropped beside her on the couch. "Want me to calculate the odds for you?"

Rebecca moved to her other side. "Pull off

some of the magic you worked to hit the lottery. The odds can't be any longer than that." She leaned around Stephanie. "Can they?"

They all snickered and Stephanie was relieved the hardest part was over. Now she had help to accomplish everything she'd imagined on the way home.

"You know, even if you're working in Lima or wherever, there's no guarantee that you make something with Daniel." Rebecca and Jen were starting to make their way out and Stephanie was dreading all the laundry that had to be done. Packing lighter for the next trip would be so much easier.

She cradled her wrist over her heart and thought about asking them to go with her to the hospital.

Tomorrow. Sleep was more important today.

"I know, Rebecca. Please don't think that's my goal here. And right now I want you to promise me that whatever happens with Daniel, you and I are friends forever. I can't live without you, and I've been doing fine without him. If I have to again, I will, but no one makes chocolate chip cookies like you do." Stephanie wished she hadn't mentioned the cookies. A cookie would have really hit the spot.

Rebecca rolled her eyes. "Please. No way is our friendship on the line, Daniel or no Daniel. Your cookie stash is safe. Just…be careful, okay? I don't want either of you hurt."

Stephanie nodded. "So, instead of thinking about him, I'm dreaming for me. Understand? I know you'll think I'm crazy, but standing in a tiny courtyard and putting on a show to introduce basic English to giggling kids was the best time I've had teaching in years. I was covered in dirt from head to toe and pretty sure getting back home would kill me, but that spark of hope and connection and feeling like I was doing what I was made for…it's wonderful and I want it. For me."

She wiped away the latest stupid tear and glanced at Jen, whose head was tilted to the side as though she was seeing Stephanie in a whole new light. "What about Paris? Or any of the other trips you've planned and talked about and outlined and *talked about* for years? This is enough to replace those dreams?"

Suddenly too weary, Stephanie rested against the doorframe. "Honestly, I think this was the dream all along. I don't think it was about a place. It was about not being afraid to take a risk. People told me I was happy and safe. Most of the time I believed them, but then there were the times that all I could think of was getting out. Trying something new. Having some adventure." She shrugged. "When this becomes commonplace, I'll move on to writing a food blog about all the bakeries in Paris. Somebody's got to do it."

Rebecca smiled and said, "You're going to make a difference in a way that a few checks will never match."

"We need the checks." Stephanie took Rebecca's hand. "That's something I didn't see before. I didn't understand your willingness to give it all away. Now I know why. That's not my way. It's your way and it's amazing. Mine is to…go. Maybe. I hope." The uncertainty that had kept her brain going in hamster-wheel circles on the plane ride popped back up. Maybe she'd never be able to convince Dr. Wright that HealthyAmericas could benefit from a communications center in Lima to support the doctors in the villages. Maybe the educational program she'd been picturing was a waste of time or money or both. Maybe there was no need for her in Lima at all.

If that was the case, she'd have her answer.

But she wasn't going to let fear keep her from trying.

For a long time her fear had been disguised as the need for safety or comfort. And the only times she'd stepped out on a limb had been for Daniel, but this she wanted for herself.

"Tomorrow I'm going to elbow my way in to meet with Dr. Wright. Once I get an invitation to the fund-raiser, we'll have to go shopping for dresses and a new car." Stephanie yawned. "What a hardship."

She wrinkled her nose at Jen who surprised them all by hugging her neck. "And I have to apply for a passport. Rebecca's coming with me." She narrowed her eyes at Rebecca. "Got it?"

Rebecca saluted. "Yes, ma'am. We'll find a doctor to give me the good stuff before it's time for Stephanie to find a place to live in Lima. We'll all have to go, if only to make sure the kitchen is up to par."

Stephanie was still wiping the tears off her face as she waved at them driving away.

She'd been afraid to tell them what she wanted.

Now she was certain she was on the right track to getting it all.

Daniel could be a part of that. Or not. The next step would be up to him.

After a good night's rest, four loads of laundry, and an X-ray to find that her wrist was sprained and her first doctor's course of action was the correct one, Stephanie was headed for Austin. She'd put on her best suit, the one she'd bought for her last job interview. It fit a little snugly around the waist, but she hoped that would help her focus. She'd tried calling ahead for an appointment, but whoever answered the phones at HealthyAmericas was very, very good.

So she'd emailed her fund-raising report to Daniel and then sent a separate email to Dr. Wright along with a note saying she'd be outside her door all afternoon. If Stephanie waited, she might falter. Being prepared for battle was good.

But when she arrived the gates were thrown open and Stephanie had to greet a welcoming Dr. Wright off balance.

When she settled across the desk from Dr. Wright, Stephanie took a deep breath, ready to launch into her three-pronged attack: first, the fund-raising she was prepared to take over in Daniel's stead at the upcoming event. Second, a hard sell for an office in Lima for a regional director and communications assistant. Third, Teresa's desire to become a permanent part of the team.

It was an extensive agenda and the time was already ticking when Dr. Wright leaned forward to pass her three tickets. "These are for the dinner we've got planned. Since Daniel's still a question mark and that usually means no, it would be great to have someone like you who's recently returned. The report you've put together is wonderful. Having a face to go with the name and the large checks you've brought in should be a powerful incentive for donors. And Daniel's going to need as much help as he can get. These programs are each impressive and a lot of work on their own. Combining them seems a bit out of reach at this point."

Stephanie had been afraid of that answer. "If you could pick one to focus on, what would be your priority?" She'd worked up several different arguments to establish herself as a necessity in Lima. The right one depended on the problem she needed to address.

"Oh, I want them all. However, it'll take fund-raising dedication like I've never seen from Daniel." Dr. Wright raised her eyebrows. "Why do I have a feeling you have the solution for that?"

Stephanie sighed happily. "Plans, I've got. With your approval, I'll get them in motion. On one condition." Dr. Wright braced her elbows on her gleaming desk. "I have this friend whose single goal is to stay in Alto and run the clinic. I'd like you to offer her a position and help me figure out how to make this work. In exchange, I'll make a difference for HealthyAmericas. On the ground in Peru and here if you need me. I will get the donations. These plans of Daniel's?" Stephanie tapped her chest. "I'm going to make them sing."

CHAPTER SIXTEEN

"OKAY, DANIEL, LAST NIGHT. You're going to have to make up your mind." Teresa slid a plate in front of him and closed his laptop. He'd been staring at the photo of Stephanie at the top of the stairs in Plata again. Her broad grin. The dust covering her from head to toe. Everything about her said victory and happiness.

Here. In Peru.

"Come with us. Dr. Wright has requested my presence at the fund-raiser since you're so grouchy about the whole thing. And Stephanie's going to have a dress for me at her hotel. Can you believe that? It's like my Cinderella moment and she's my fairy god-mother." Teresa slid into the chair next to him and started reorganizing the towering pile of files he needed to put away before they left for Lima. "Is staring at her photo going to help make the decision?"

"Probably not." He took a few bites of excellent noodle-y casserole and watched her ruthlessly organize his mess.

"What would?" Teresa put one elbow on the table and propped her chin on her hand. "Do I need to get your sister to ask?"

If anyone could get him home, it would be Rebecca. But she'd never ask because she knew how much being here meant to him.

Daniel wasn't really wrestling with the decision to go back to Texas at this point. If he didn't get on a plane, he'd be disgusted with himself. HealthyAmericas needed him. Stephanie was there. Only one thing would hold him back, but he wasn't going to give in to fear at this point.

That didn't mean he was happy or comfortable with the idea. Not yet.

"Come with me." Teresa grabbed his hand and pulled. His fork clattered to the plate and he followed her out into the shadowed street. Bright light from Alto's store spilled across the road.

Daniel was fishing in his pockets for coins

because there was definitely a Coke in his future when Teresa called out, *"Hola!"* Tamaya waved, accepted his money and then gave him a Coke.

Teresa marched over to the small laptop in the corner. When he could get an internet connection he'd been haunting Facebook, scanning for updates and checking his email for any small bit of news from home.

The keys clicked as Teresa typed in a web address.

"I sent Dr. Wright a letter with my recommendation that you be a permanent addition to the team. We'll work out the terms once I get her approval, but I won't stop asking." Daniel hadn't told her because he hadn't wanted to get her hopes up, but she deserved to know how much he appreciated her.

Teresa glanced over her shoulder. "Thanks, boss. That should help. I've got an advocate on the ground in Austin, too."

She meant Stephanie. Of course she did. They'd bonded as quickly as everyone bonded with Stephanie, and Stephanie was a loyal friend, one who'd go to bat.

"Stop thinking. Read." He tried to grab

the Coke Teresa had snatched from his hand, but she was too fast for him. He heaved a disgusted sigh and sat down to read.

"What is this? A Peru blog?" He had no need to read about the place, but the pictures were familiar. As he read the posts Stephanie had written while she was with him, he was impressed with the sparkling optimism that lined each sentence. She had loved this place. Her writing showed it. The photographs made it clear why.

The new posts were all about the efforts of HealthyAmericas, and there was a big splash about the upcoming fund-raiser. "Black tie. Of course." The added bonus was the guest of honor, the administrator of Holly Heights Hospital. "Being honored for sponsoring a science education program in rural Peruvian schools." He had to read the paragraph more than once for it to all sink in. The same administrator who'd slashed his mentoring program was being honored by HealthyAmericas. Eventually Teresa handed him back his Coke.

"She's amazing." Teresa crossed her arms over her chest. "You know that, right? You'd be an idiot to let a woman like that go."

Daniel took a deep, satisfying drink. "Well, we both know I can be an idiot. But it's not a terminal case."

"Whether you go or stay, she's making plans to come back. You saw that, right? Stephanie's not afraid of the conditions or the overwhelming list of needs here." Teresa pointed at her last post on the mountain. "She's still got a lot of work to do."

"And if she had some help in Texas she could get back to it sooner." He watched Teresa's eyes widen and then she whooped in celebration. Tamaya's eyes got even bigger. "Before we leave in the morning I need a quick meeting at the school."

Teresa clapped and cheered. "Sure thing. I'm with you, boss. Are we about to make a grand gesture?"

"I'm going to do my best. You can be *my* fairy godmother." He was going to get his own message up, through the power of social media, one that would make sure Stephanie knew where he stood.

THE HOTEL IN Austin was beautiful, not that Stephanie had seen much of it. She'd rented a gorgeous suite where she, Rebecca and Jen had had the most luxurious slumber party of all time.

The room, the night and the beautiful gown Stephanie had chosen for herself were dreams come true.

Teresa breezed in an hour before the HealthyAmericas party started. Rebecca peppered her with questions about the clinics and her brother. Jen and Stephanie did their best to make sure everyone made it to the event on time—not an easy feat when there was a Jacuzzi tub, champagne and room service to keep them all occupied.

As they were about to leave, Teresa stopped and said, "Oh, wait. I have a gift for you from Daniel."

Rebecca's face lit up and Teresa offered her a cell phone. Instead of being happy Daniel had sent his sister—her best friend—a message, she was shaken. He didn't seem to be thinking of her as much as she was thinking of him. There had been no personal emails. No Facebook statuses where she might read between the lines.

"Oh. How sweet."

A bitter frown almost made it to her face, which confused Stephanie. Daniel wasn't sentimental. He'd always do the honorable thing. Expecting a message from him was silly.

Besides, she wasn't living for him. Everything she did now was for her own benefit.

"Snap out of it." Jen shoved the phone in her hand. "Don't you want to see your gift?"

Stephanie took the phone in self-defense. The picture on the screen was from Daniel's Facebook page. He was standing in front of the school in Alto, all the students in their school uniforms surrounding him. His hand-lettered sign read "We miss you, Stephanie." The kids all looked happy but Daniel was serious.

She shoved the phone back at Teresa and pinched her nose to keep the tears at bay. "Oh, man, if my mascara runs…" She shrugged. "I won't even care. Thank you. I'm going to make this work. He's worth it. They're worth it. Let's go make lots and lots of money."

She felt like a conquering general when they paused inside the doorway to the hotel's ballroom. HealthyAmericas had put up posters showing the work of all the doctors in South America. The room was brightly lit

and all the people in it were dressed spectacularly. She should have felt so out of place,
but she'd defeated the hike to Plata.

This should be no problem.

Teresa, Rebecca and Jen all had their
marching orders. "Let's do this." They split
up and started a well-coordinated attack on
the wealthy of southeast Texas.

It was difficult to measure success, but
if she counted the number of stories she'd
told, pictures she'd taken and introductions
she'd made to Dr. Wright, Stephanie was
pretty sure she and her team were winning
this fight. All the programs she wanted were
expensive, but it wouldn't take much to get
the ball rolling. She had enough favors to
call in that she could work with very little.

In order to strengthen her attack, she hit
the buffet, carefully selecting the most beautiful and largest piece of cheesecake she
could find.

"I was wondering if you could introduce
me to Stephanie Yates. I hear she's changing the world."

Stephanie slowly turned to see Daniel

standing behind her, his hair damp and his suit tight across the shoulders.

"Tall. Blonde. Usually covered in dirt. Prettiest smile you've ever seen."

A million things ran through her head. None of them mattered more than getting her arms around him right that second. His little grunt as he caught her should have been embarrassing, but she was way past that.

"You came. I can't believe it." She blinked rapidly to will away the tears that were about to spill over.

Daniel didn't answer, just tightened his arms around her, his hands hot against her bare back. He was real. He was here. He'd come home.

"Wait. You're going back, aren't you?" She leaned away from him. Now she was committed to Peru. He was too, right?

"Of course, but I know how much quicker and easier the work is when you have some help." He rolled his eyes. "Not that you need my help, because you are obviously the fund-raising rock star, but I want you back as soon as possible. So I'm helping."

Rebecca and Jen came running up with

Tom Jenkins, the graying administrator of Holly Heights Hospital, in tow. Stephanie tensed, ready to go on the defensive. She just wasn't sure who she was protecting.

Before Daniel could address that problem, he had to untangle himself from his sister's tight grip. She was crying and laughing. "You jerk. Why didn't you tell us you were coming?" They all turned to stare at Teresa who shrugged. "Sorry. He wanted a grand entrance."

Daniel frowned at her and then held his hand out to the man who'd sent him packing. "Tom. It's good to see you. I wanted to thank you in person for your grant to help the education program."

The two men shook hands. "Once Stephanie made her passionate, well-thought-out case, we couldn't do anything but write a check. The board unanimously agreed. That doesn't happen often."

"She's the expert. She'll do a great job." Daniel wrapped one arm around Stephanie and the other around Rebecca. "I'd like to spend a minute with the woman of the hour. If it's okay, I'll bring her back to you."

"Sure, Daniel." Tom turned to go, but stopped. "Listen, all that… I'm glad to see the work you're doing in Peru. People make mistakes. I'm glad to have a chance to make a better decision this time. Your program at Holly Heights Hospital would have been good for the community."

Stephanie hadn't realized how hard she was squeezing Daniel's hand until he untangled his fingers and flexed them before he set his hand on her hip. "That was a mistake, but nothing like my arrogant attack on you. I regret that, even if I can't regret where it's led me."

Tom shifted toward Daniel. "Sure. And maybe I'll do a survey, see what people think about a small mentoring program."

Rebecca cleared her throat. "Luckily, I am the perfect person to help there, Mr. Jenkins. Come with us. We'll…uh, we'll go find food. We can chat. Okay?" She grabbed Jen and Teresa and pulled them toward the buffet table.

Daniel wrapped his arms around Stephanie's waist. "I hear you're making big plans for Lima. A communications office, a central spot for storage and a jump-off point for doctors leaving for different areas."

"Yes, with or without you, though. I want to make that clear. This shouldn't have any impact on your decision about us or dating or—"

Daniel pressed his lips against hers in a sweet kiss hello. As he held her in his arms, the strange feeling that no matter where she went, she'd be home and safe and happy as long as he was there settled over her. When the kiss went beyond a mere hello, the quiet gasps and whispers finally got her attention.

She was smiling as she stepped back and pressed one finger over her mouth. "I guess that answers my question."

"I learn from my mistakes, Steph. Not only do I want to take you to dinner, I desperately need your help to make my work a success. The people in Alto and Plata and Manzana miss you. I miss you, and together we're going to make this work. Here in Texas, there in Peru, we belong together. I understand that now."

She held up her hand, her wrist unwrapped but still tender. "Think you'll be able to work without worrying?"

"That will take some practice." Daniel

pressed his forehead to hers. "So you'll understand why I don't let you out of my sight for a few months. Or years, right?"

"What a sacrifice. For you, I'll make it." Stephanie had to bite her lip to contain the tears of joy threatening to spill out in front of all the donors she'd intended to charm. "You know, it takes you a while to warm up to the romantic gestures, but you really make up for lost time."

He watched her closely. "Put me out of my misery. Tell me you love me."

She raised her eyebrows. "Here in Texas, we'll go by my rules and I say…you first."

"Gladly. I love you. Have for a long time. Thank you for proving me wrong."

Stephanie laughed. "Now I know it's real, this love thing. I love you and this adventure. I can't wait to see what comes next."

* * * * *

*Don't miss the next book in
Cheryl Harper's*
LUCKY NUMBERS
miniseries, available October 2015!

LARGER-PRINT BOOKS!

GET 2 FREE
LARGER-PRINT NOVELS
PLUS 2 FREE
MYSTERY GIFTS

Love Inspired®

Larger-print novels are now available...

YES! Please send me 2 FREE LARGER-PRINT Love Inspired® novels and my 2 FREE mystery gifts (gifts are worth about $10). After receiving them, if I don't wish to receive any more books, I can return the shipping statement marked "cancel." If I don't cancel, I will receive 6 brand-new novels every month and be billed just $5.49 per book in the U.S. or $5.99 per book in Canada. That's a savings of at least 19% off the cover price. It's quite a bargain! Shipping and handling is just 50¢ per book in the U.S. and 75¢ per book in Canada.* I understand that accepting the 2 free books and gifts places me under no obligation to buy anything. I can always return a shipment and cancel at any time. Even if I never buy another book, the two free books and gifts are mine to keep forever.

122/322 IDN GH6D

Name	(PLEASE PRINT)

Address	Apt. #

City	State/Prov.	Zip/Postal Code

Signature (if under 18, a parent or guardian must sign)

Mail to the **Reader Service**:
IN U.S.A.: P.O. Box 1867, Buffalo, NY 14240-1867
IN CANADA: P.O. Box 609, Fort Erie, Ontario L2A 5X3

**Are you a current subscriber to Love Inspired® books
and want to receive the larger-print edition?
Call 1-800-873-8635 or visit www.ReaderService.com.**

* Terms and prices subject to change without notice. Prices do not include applicable taxes. Sales tax applicable in N.Y. Canadian residents will be charged applicable taxes. Offer not valid in Quebec. This offer is limited to one order per household. Not valid to current subscribers to Love Inspired Larger-Print books. All orders subject to credit approval. Credit or debit balances in a customer's account(s) may be offset by any other outstanding balance owed by or to the customer. Please allow 4 to 6 weeks for delivery. Offer available while quantities last.

Your Privacy—The Reader Service is committed to protecting your privacy. Our Privacy Policy is available online at www.ReaderService.com or upon request from the Reader Service.

We make a portion of our mailing list available to reputable third parties that offer products we believe may interest you. If you prefer that we not exchange your name with third parties, or if you wish to clarify or modify your communication preferences, please visit us at www.ReaderService.com/consumerschoice or write to us at Reader Service Preference Service, P.O. Box 9062, Buffalo, NY 14240-9062. Include your complete name and address.

LILP15